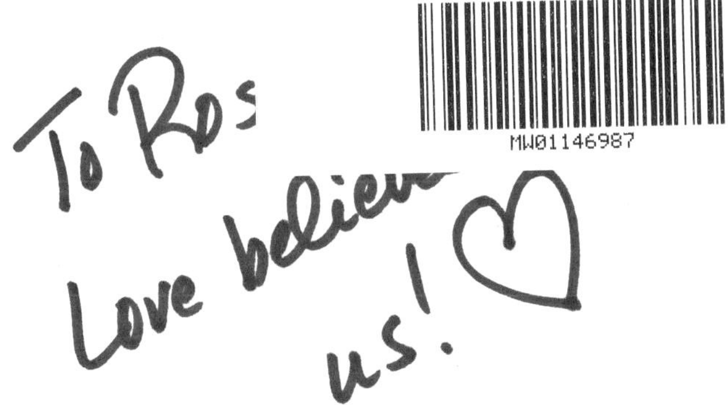

BEAST

A Lords of Carnage MC Romance

DAPHNE LOVELING

ISBN-13:
978-1987700336

ISBN-10:
1987700333

This book is a work of fiction.

Any similarity to persons living or dead is purely coincidental.

The FBI field office in Cleveland that figures in these pages, and all the agents associated with it, is a complete fabrication that exists only in the imagination of the author.

Cover Photo by Lebedev Roman
Olegovich/Shutterstock.com
Cover Design by Coverlüv

CONTENTS

For Cintina.

I wish you could have read this book.

1
BEAST

The loud bang behind makes the woman behind the counter shriek in alarm and drop her phone.

"Holy shit!" she yelps. Her eyes bug wide as they dart to me.

"Jesus, Beast!" she gasps. "You scared the living hell out of me!"

"Sorry about that," I shrug. "You really need to get that screen door fixed."

Hannah takes a deep breath and lets out a noisy sigh of relief. "Tell me about it." The blood slowly begins to return to her face. "It's been like that for over a week. Chance keeps saying he'll do something about it. But clearly, it's pretty low on his priority list." She glances toward the back of the shop with an irritated frown. "Then again, he's not out here listening to it day in and day out, like I am."

"He around?" I ask. "I can bitch at him if you want."

"Nah. He's not coming in until later on today." Hannah cocks her head at me. "Wait — your appointment wasn't with him, was it?"

"Nope. With Dez."

"Oh, good." She looks relieved. "I was worried Chance fucked up."

"Not on this front, at least."

Chance Armstrong is the owner here at Rebel Ink. This shop is one of half a dozen tattoo places in the area, but it's the only the Lords of Carnage will go to. The artists here are top notch, and they've been doing all our work for years.

I've known Chance since he was a little kid. He was a few years behind me in school. I can still remember him way back then: a geeky kid with stick-out ears and glasses. This was long before tattoos snarled the surface of his skin from the neck down. He's come a long way since then. This place is known throughout the region as the best ink shop around.

I'm here to get some new ink on a faded tattoo. Normally, I don't bother with touch-ups. But this one is special. It's the first one I ever got. It's the head of a snarling beast, with a mouth full of flame. The orange of the fire has dimmed, and it's time to get it back in shape.

"Dez is in his room," Hannah says, nodding toward the hall. "You can go on back."

"Thanks."

I head down to find him in his studio. He's hunched over a sketch pad, busily working on a design. His dark beard covers the entire lower half of his face. An elastic band pulls his long hair back out of his way. Dez looks up at my footsteps, grunts a greeting, and sets the pad down without a word. He isn't known for his sparkling conversation. It's one of the things I like about him.

I lift my chin at him and sit down in the chair opposite him without preamble.

"Touching up today?" he murmurs.

I nod. "The flames," I tell him. "Do what you want with the rest."

I pull off my shirt to give him access to the tat, which is on my left pec. He peers at it for a few seconds, even though he knows it well. "I'll touch up the outline, some of the details," he tells me. "Keep the overall look of it. The blur of the old ink is actually an asset. Adds to the character."

I settle in, watching silently as he preps his instruments. When he's ready, I just lie back and let him work. For a long time, the only sound in the room the tattoo gun and the occasional rustle as he shifts position.

Dez works with a furrowed brow. Time passes. I mostly zone out, aware of the pain almost like a meditation.

"All done," he eventually says. He pulls back and grabs a hand mirror for me so I can take a look.

The beast has recovered his snarl. I flex the muscle and grin. "Looks good."

"Thanks, man." Dez nods briefly. He's not great at accepting compliments, but I can tell he appreciates it anyway.

"How's the fam?" I ask as he grabs the ointment to put over the new ink.

He nods. "Okay. Stacey's been sick a lot lately. Strep. Docs think she may need to get her tonsils out, but they're holding off for now 'cause she's so young. Carrie's been off work a lot to stay home with her."

"That sucks."

"Yeah." He shrugs. "She's takin' it in stride. Luckily her boss is being cool about it. She's trying to get a lot of work done at home while Stacey's asleep."

I watch Dez place the bandage and try to imagine him at home with a girlfriend and a kid. It's not easy. But I guess most people would look at my brothers in the club and not believe that lots of them have kids as well. I've seen guys tough enough to make a grown man piss his pants, down on the floor playing horsey with a two year-old. So, I know dads come in all sorts of shapes and sizes. And some of the best ones I know are covered head to toe in ink.

Not me, of course. That's never gonna happen.

I make a mental note to toss a few extra bucks in Dez's direction by way of a tip, and shake his hand as I get up to leave. Then the two of us head back down the hall.

Hannah's staring into space when we get to the reception area. Her phone is lying on the desk in front of her. Her face is pale, and her jaw is clenching and unclenching, like she's trying to keep her emotions in check. When she notices us, she quickly sits up and flashes the two of us an unconvincing smile.

"All set?" she croaks, her eyes flickering from me to Dez.

"Yeah." Dez gives her a quick nod and tells her what to charge me for, then lifts a finger at me and turns back toward his studio.

Hanna grabs my ticket to ring me up. She takes a ragged breath and sniffles, and I realize she's either been crying or trying not to.

"Hey, you still freaked out about that door slamming?" I ask, a little alarmed. "Shit, if it's getting to you that much, I can grab some tools and fix it for you."

"No, no." She shakes her head and sniffles again, then looks up at me apologetically. "It's not that. I'm just… I just got a text from my aunt. My little cousin has been missing for a few days." Her voice begins to quaver on the last word, and she swallows and tries again. "She… just kind of disappeared into thin air. Didn't come home from school last Thursday. We have no idea where she could be." Her chin trembles. "She's only fifteen," she whispers.

"Shit, Hannah. I'm sorry." Fuck, no wonder she looks like hell. She must be worried sick.

I cast about in my stupid lizard brain for something to say that won't just make her feel even worse. "Have you, uh, talked to the cops?" I finally ask.

I'm pretty sure it's the first time in my life I've ever asked that question.

Hannah snorts wetly. "Yeah," she says in disgust. "My aunt has been down to the station a couple of times. They just ask how she knows Zoe didn't just run away?" Hannah fixes me with an angry, intense stare. "She *didn't* run away!" she cries. "But even so, what if she did? She's still missing, and she's still only fifteen! How can they not even care enough to *look* for her?"

I hold her gaze and don't look away. She's right, of course. It's fucking bullshit. But I know enough about cops — especially the cops in fuckin' Tanner Springs — to know they pick and choose what they respond to. They're not about to give a family like Hannah's, from the wrong side of the tracks, the time of day. They're too busy kissing the ass of our piece of shit mayor, Jarred Holloway. The patrol cars in our city spend a shitload of time cruising around and ticketing loitering teenagers in the tony part of town during the daylight, so the rich folks can see them Keeping Crime Off the Streets. They don't touch the real shit with a ten-foot pole. The domestic violence calls at 3 a.m. The petty drug dealers who sell to poor kids who've got nothing in their lives and are just looking for an escape.

And Hannah Crescent's little cousin? I'm sure as shit she isn't even on the Tanner Springs P.D.'s radar. Their family hasn't given enough campaign money to Mayor Holloway for them to rate.

I wish I had something positive to say, but I don't. So I don't say anything at all. She seems to realize the information she's revealed is too personal, and her eyes quickly flick down toward the desk. "I'm sorry," she whispers. "It's not your concern."

"Don't be sorry, Hannah." I cast about again some more. "She'll turn up." I find myself saying. Which is probably true.

One way or another.

Hannah gives me the saddest fucking look I've ever seen. "I hope so. She's like a little sister to me, Beast. And my poor aunt..." She shakes her head. "She's going out of her mind. Zoe's her only child."

"I can imagine." Fuck, I sound like a goddamn moron. I lean on the counter and give her my money, with a generous tip for Dez. Straightening, I say, "I'm sorry. I hope she turns up soon."

"Thanks, Beast." She gives me a tremulous smile.

I walk out of Rebel Ink feeling pissed off and unsettled. I've known Hannah for years. Even though she's only an acquaintance, the thought of her little cousin, or any fifteen year-old girl for that matter — out there somewhere, lost and alone — gets to me more than I'd like. I didn't say this to Hannah, but I wonder if she's even in the area anymore. The possibilities are endless. She could have run away, like the cops said. She could have been taken. Hell, she could have just gone wandering around out in the country somewhere and gotten lost, though I can't imagine a kid that age wouldn't have a cell phone nowadays.

Shaking the thoughts from my head, I cross the parking lot to my bike and straddle the seat. It's early afternoon, and I'm on my way to Twisted Pipes, my club's custom bike and auto shop. Hawk's got a few projects on deadline and a couple of the guys are out sick, so I said I'd come help him out.

I'm just getting ready to fire up the bike when my phone buzzes in my pocket. Thinking it might be Hawk, I grab it and glance at the screen. It's a call, not a text, and it's Gunner.

"Hey," I bark into the phone.

"Hey, brother." Gunner's voice is tinny on the other end. "You got time to do me a favor?"

"What's up?"

I hear him take a drag on a cigarette and blow it out. That must mean he's stressed. He's mostly quit the cancer sticks since his old lady, Alix, got pregnant. "I got a problem. A *Lemmy* problem."

I suppress a laugh. "I see. What's up?"

Gunner sighs. "Apparently he's out causing trouble downtown. I got a call from Zeb over at the Lion's Tap saying Lemmy's bein' drunk and disorderly outside. I don't want him to get hauled in, but I don't have time to go get him. I'm on my way to take Alix for her doctor's appointment."

I nod at the phone. Alix is eight months along, and big enough that she looks ready to pop at any moment.

"Okay, I'll take care of it. I'm just coming out of Rebel Ink. I'll head over there right now."

"Thanks, brother. I owe you one."

"As long as that 'one' is a bottle of my favorite whiskey, you're on."

Gunner chuckles. "I don't owe you *that* much."

I smirk. "Let's see how much damage control I have to do. Talk to ya. Say hi to Alix."

"Will do."

I end the call and fire up the bike. Then I head out of the parking lot toward downtown, wondering what kind of scene I'll find when I get there.

2
BROOKE

The tumbling Styrofoam cup of coffee spares the stack of papers on my desk, unloading its entire contents on the pants of my navy suit instead.

"God *flaming* dammit!" I hiss as I jump to my feet, wincing as the hot liquid burns through to my skin. I only managed to take a few sips before I overturned the whole damn thing on myself. Grabbing the handle of my desk's bottom drawer, I wrench it open to find my gym bag. I unzip it and pull out a ratty towel, which I throw on the spreading pool beside my rolling chair and start swishing it around with my foot.

"Careful, there."

Lafontaine's slightly condescending voice tells me he's right behind me. Inwardly I cringe, and just stop myself from groaning in frustration. So, not only am I going to look like crap all day *and* smell like a convenience store, but my boss just happened to witness the whole stupid episode. Awesome.

"Yeah," I murmur. I turn to him and try a carefree chuckle. "Just my luck, too. I really needed the caffeine this morning."

"Something wrong?" Lafontaine asks, raising a critical eyebrow at me.

I suppose it's not too surprising that a special agent with the FBI would take every innocuous remark as an opportunity to glean information. Lafontaine has probably never had a casual conversation in his life. But even so, he's reading entirely too much into a simple accident. I'd love to tell him that to his face. Unfortunately, I've learned from experience that he doesn't take kindly to suggestions from underlings. No matter how small.

"Oh, no, no," I reply hastily. I can't afford to let him get the impression I'm not operating on all cylinders. "I just, ah, worked out extra hard at the gym this morning."

"I see," he replies. The frown he gives me implies he doesn't quite believe me, but thankfully he lets it go. "Agent Brentano, I'd like to see you in my office, please. Five minutes." He looks down at me in thinly veiled distaste. "I'll give you a chance to clean yourself up first."

Fuck. "Right away, sir."

The echo of his heels tap judgmentally down the hallway. Growling to myself, I grab my purse from the top drawer and book it down to the restrooms, leaving the towel to soak up the rest of the spill. The whole way there, I'm muttering to myself, but stop abruptly when a coworker tapping on a laptop looks up at me with a confused glance.

Special Agent Craig Lafontaine has been my boss since I've been at this FBI field office in Cleveland, just a hair short of four years. He's almost exactly what you'd expect the director of an FBI field office to be like from watching the movies: a man of indeterminate age, well built and in shape without looking like a weight lifter. Hair the color of cardboard, cut short with a side part so straight you could use it as a ruler in a pinch. A face that's blandly handsome and naturally devoid of expression, which makes him perfectly disconcerting to have a conversation with. It serves him well during interrogations. It's not so great when you're working under him, though.

In the time I've known Lafontaine, I've learned essentially nothing about him as a person. I don't know anything about his hobbies, private life, or likes and dislikes. I have no idea whether he's married, or has kids. And I realize that's by design. Lafontaine is the consummate career FBI guy.

And even though he's never said it in so many words, I've always gotten the distinct feeling that he doesn't love having a woman working for him.

Four minutes later, I've managed to mostly mop myself off and used the hand-dryer on the wettest part of my pant leg. I stand in front of Agent Lafontaine's closed door and give it three quick taps with my knuckle. I think I hear a murmur, but I'm not quite sure. A couple of seconds later, he barks, "Come in, I said!" Feeling my face flush, I reach for the knob and walk inside.

"Take a seat."

He's frowning at his monitor, and doesn't look at me at first. I do as he says. I sit patiently, taking deep but quiet breaths and doing my best to project self-assuredness. Eventually he raps sharply on a key and turns to me, leaning back in his chair.

"I've got a case for you," he says without preamble.

"Okay." I'm relieved at the normalcy of his news. But it feels weird. I can't quite figure out why he acted like I was about to be reprimanded if this was all he wanted to tell me.

Lafontaine glances down at his normally pristine desk, and I notice there's a manila folder on it. It's thin for an FBI case folder: barely an eighth of an inch thick. "Take a look," he says.

I reach forward and slide it toward me. He's silent as I open it and begin to skim the top sheet. "An HT case?" I ask, glancing at him.

He gives the barest of nods. "We've had a tip come in. A town southeast of here, where we don't have a resident agency." He shifts slightly in his seat. "I want you to go down and check it out. See if there's any credibility to it."

"What's the town?" I look down at the file again.

"Tanner Springs."

My eyes freeze on the page. My whole body goes rigid. Every nerve ending is alert.

I try as hard as I can not to let a single flicker of emotion show on my face.

"You grew up there. Right?"

He asks, but it's not a question. He knows. Of course he knows. The background investigation process to become an FBI agent is incredibly thorough. The agency knows practically everything about me: my family, where I was born, my education, my associates. They know my credit history, my mental and physical health history, whether I've ever lived outside of the country, and who I went to my senior prom with.

(Trick question. I didn't go to my senior prom.)

"Uh-huh," I murmur, even though it's not necessary. Inside my head, I can hear the rushing of blood as it pounds through my ears.

"Review the file. You'll head down to the location, interview the parties concerned, and assess the viability of the situation."

"What kind of tips have there been?" I manage to croak out. My voice sounds tight in my throat, like I'm not getting enough air. I focus on my breathing, in and out, hoping it will calm my nerves.

"It's one tip. A shop owner, in particular. Owns a sub shop in a mini-mall in town. Apparently, one of the other businesses in the mall, a laundromat, has a lot of foot traffic lately. Mostly men." He snorts softly. "The complaint he filed said these men are inside for a long time, but none of them ever come into his shop to grab a sandwich. His business has gone down. He thinks there's something suspicious going on, and he's convinced it's a front for a human trafficking operation."

"That's all?" I'm perplexed. It doesn't seem like enough to go on for Lafontaine to want to follow up on it.

He frowns. "This not a big enough case for you, Agent Brentano?" There's an edge in his voice.

"No, no, not at all," I stammer.

"Orders from on high," he barks. "The agency has been dinged one too many times recently for not following up on tips that ended up having merit. Until further notice, the protocol is to follow up on all tips of certain types, no matter their source."

Ah. I get it.

Cover your ass.

I'm just going out there to show that Lafontaine did his due diligence.

"Wouldn't it possibly be sufficient to interview the person who left the tip by phone?" I suggest, hoping against hope.

As soon as Lafontaine's hard stare meets mine, I know that's the wrong answer.

"What's the matter, Brentano?" he snaps. "Are you too important for this job? Who knows, maybe you'll crack open a major case, and Philadelphia will snap you up."

Oh, shit.

I think I know why Lafontaine is giving me this case. It's punishment. He knows I've been angling for a transfer to Philly.

And as much as he doesn't love having me around, I'm guessing he'd like it even less if I got what would amount to a promotion.

My stomach sours at the thought that he knows *exactly* what he's sending me out for. He *can't* know all of it, though — there's no way even the bureau's background check process could dig *that* deep into my past. So I have to assume that he just thinks he's sending me on a fool's errand to a podunk town that I just happen to have grown up in.

And goddamnit, as much as I don't want to go, I'm not about to give him the satisfaction of knowing just how much I *don't* want to take this assignment. I will shut my trap, suck this up, and do my damn job. No matter how much I am dreading it.

"Not at all, sir. I'll get right on it."

"Take the file. You'll leave tomorrow." Lafontaine swivels in his chair and turns back toward his computer monitor. The message is clear: we're done here.

"Thank you," I say. I scoop up the file and rise to leave. Back out in the hallway, I let out the breath I realize I've been holding and stare down at the folder.

Son of a bitch.

* * *

That night — after stopping at the dry cleaner on the way home for a rush job on my navy pants — I sit on my couch in my dingy one-bedroom apartment and stare at the pages of the file. A glass of wine sits on the low table in front of me. Next to me on the other cushion, my guinea pig Walter grapples with a half-carrot I've given him, making soft *wheek wheek* sounds of contentment.

There's not much more information in here than I already knew when I left Lafontaine's office. For the dozenth time, I tell myself he's sending me on a wild goose chase. But that's irrelevant. I still have a job to do.

"This is bullshit, Walter," I tell him. "You know that?"

But Walter doesn't answer, mesmerized as he is by the carrot.

I sigh and haul myself up to my feet. I'm going to have to pack my bag tonight if I want to head out of town tomorrow morning. But first, I have to get Walter a pig-sitter.

I flip the deadbolt lock to my apartment, then wander outside and knock on a door at the end of the hall. A few minutes later, a pint-sized twelve year-old answers.

"Lily," I say. "Can you do me a favor and take care of Walter for a few days?"

Lily breaks into a wide, gap-toothed grin. The braces she recently had put on will take care of that eventually, and to tell the truth, it will break my heart. "Sure!" she cries excitedly. "I'm sure my mom won't mind. Mo-o-om!"

Lily races inside her apartment, and then a few moments later races back. "Mom says it's okay!"

"Thanks, Gretchen!" I call out. "I owe you one!"

"Don't mention it!" a voice calls back.

"Come on," I say to Lily, holding open the door for her to come out. "I'm leaving early tomorrow, so let's bring him over now."

Lily follows me back to my place, helps me corral Walter, and listens patiently as I go over instructions she's heard already from previous pig-sitting gigs. Together we carry his cage and food back to her place, get him set up in her bedroom, and I tell her I'll see her when I get back. I thank Gretchen again, and walk back to my apartment, noticing as I always do how strangely quiet it seems without Walter around.

I settle back in on the couch to finish my wine and mentally go over what I need to pack with me. I might be gone for a week or more, so I'd better err on the side of having enough clothing to go that long without doing laundry. As I'm going through my pack list in my head, I realize I haven't made a hotel reservation in Tanner Springs yet. I grab my laptop and start the process of booking a room for myself with my government credit card. It's unlikely places would be full up in a town that size, but still, I'm a planner. I'd rather have my sleeping arrangements taken care of before I get there.

I pull up a search for "hotels Tanner Springs." The first hit is for a chain hotel I don't remember being there the last time I was in town. I click on it and look at the address, trying to imagine in my mind's eye where the hotel must be. There used to be a city park there, I think.

My stomach starts to feel a little unsettled as it hits me that I'm really going back. This time tomorrow, I'll be in the town where I grew up, for the first time since the day I turned eighteen years old.

Suddenly, I'm a little afraid I'm going to throw up.

Stop it, I tell myself crossly. *This isn't high school anymore. You're not the same person. You're just doing your job. You'll get in and get out, and that will be it. You don't want to do it, but you'll be fine.*

And it *will* be fine. It has to be.

For better or for worse, I'm going to Tanner Springs. I've got a job to do. And I'm damn well going to do it.

3
BEAST

Hannah's still preoccupying me as I ride toward downtown. I'm half a block away from the Lion's Tap when I see a thin, unsteady figure shambling around in front of the bar.

"Christ," I mutter, but the word's drowned out by the noise of my engine. Pulling into an empty parking space in front of the bar, I cut the motor and call out a name. "Lemmy!"

After a second, the figure slows and turns around to peer at me.

Lemmy's not his real name. I'm not sure most people in Tanner Springs even know his real name anymore. Except for family, of which he has little. Once upon a time, he bore a fair resemblance to Lemmy Kilmister, the front man for Motörhead. He played up the similarity, letting his hair grow long like the rocker's, and the nickname stuck. These days, about the only thing that's left of that resemblance are the wispy gray muttonchops he still sports on his sunken cheeks.

I climb off the bike and stride toward him. I haven't seen Lemmy in a while, but he looks even worse than usual. His eyes are bloodshot as hell, and a blood vessel has burst in one of them. His mud-colored T-shirt hasn't been washed in several days, and he smells like whiskey and piss. He's emaciated to the point of starvation. Inwardly, I wince.

"What?" Lemmy barks in confusion. "I just came out here for a smoke," he slurs, pointing a gnarled finger toward the bar. "Have a smoke with me, Beast. Then come on inside and have a drink."

"A little early for me, Lem."

"Naaaahhh!" he wheezes, waving his hand in front of him to swat away the ridiculous idea. A haze of alcohol breath wafts toward me, and I take a step back. "Isss five a'clock, somewheres!" He starts to cackle uproariously at his own joke.

The door to the bar opens and Zeb comes out. "Hey, Beast. Gunner call you?"

"Yeah." I watch as Zeb flashes Lemmy an irritated look. "How long's he been here?" I ask.

"Long enough," Zeb answers wryly.

The door's opening seems to have made Lemmy forget about having a smoke. He lurches forward to catch it while it's still open. "C'mon," he wheezes. "Less have a drink. On me."

Zeb snorts. "You ran out of money half an hour ago, old man."

"Come on, Lemmy," I say, catching him by the arm. "I got a better idea. Let's go get something to eat. Sop up some of that alcohol."

"Nawww…" he protests. Luckily, as bad a drunk as Lemmy is, he's not a mean one, so he doesn't get mad or try to take a swing at me. The last thing I want to do is hurt the poor fucker.

"Yeah. Come on. There's plenty of time to get a drink later." I tighten the grip on his skinny bicep and start to lead him away. "See ya, Zeb."

"Thanks, Beast." Zeb casts a glance at Lemmy that's both sympathetic and exasperated. "Appreciate it."

"No problem."

I pull Lemmy down the street, barely listening to his drunken murmurs of objection. I'm on my bike, so I can't drive him anywhere. He's far too drunk to be able to balance on the back of it. I manage to keep him talking and take him in the direction of the Downtown Diner, just down the block.

I get him in the door, and settle him in at one of the faded leatherette booths. Once I'm sure he's not gonna tip over, I go grab one of the waitresses, a middle-aged woman named Penny.

"Hey, Lemmy could use a good meal," I tell her. I reach into my pocket and pull out a bill. "Grab him something with a shitload of carbs, and a pot of hot coffee, will ya?"

"You're a good egg, Beast."

"Don't let it get around. I got my reputation to protect."

She snorts. "Don't worry. Your secret's safe with me."

I wait with Lemmy until Penny's got a pot of joe in front of him. Then I go outside to call Gunner and let him know I've got his uncle in hand. He tells me he'll be on his way over with a car to take Lemmy home just as soon as Alix's appointment with the doc is finished.

When I come back into the diner, the owner, a fat fuck of a man named Dick Dawson, waddles toward me with anger in his beady, squinty little eyes.

"What in God's name are you doing bringing a drunk in here?" he wheezes self-importantly. I flick my eyes over to Penny, who's looking at me apologetically. I'm guessing she got an earful from this tub of shit about letting Lemmy sit down.

No good deed goes unpunished, I think to myself. For fuck's sake.

I raise myself up to my full six feet and seven inches. "Would you care to repeat that?" I rumble.

Dickless blanches but doesn't back down. "This is a private establishment," he stammers. He tries to stand taller, too, but all it does is cause his gut to hang out further over his belt buckle. "As the owner, I reserve the right to refuse service to anyone I choose."

"Fair enough," I say easily. A couple of the other customers have turned to watch our conversation. "And as Lemmy's friend and temporary guardian, I reserve the right to beat the shit out of anyone who denies him some fucking coffee and lunch."

"I'll have the cops called on you," Dickless chokes out. All the color is draining from his fat face, but I have to give him points for trying.

I shrug. "Not fast enough. By the time they get here, you'll already be picking your teeth up off the floor."

"Let him have some goddamn coffee, Dick!" one of the other customers calls out.

"Nah! I wanna see a fight!" someone else replies.

"Not gonna be much of a fight, I don't think," a third one says. A wave of laughter flows through the diner.

"He may be right, *Dick*," I murmur, taking a step forward. He instantly moves back, instinctively crossing his arms in front of him. "Not sure you're gonna last very long against me. What's it gonna be?"

Dickless purses his lips and shoots a quick glance toward Lemmy's booth. "Just… make sure he doesn't cause any trouble." He turns on his heel and walks away, past Penny and into the kitchen. A chorus of hoots and catcalls follows him.

I walk up to Penny and hand her another bill. "This is for having to deal with that asshole," I mutter.

She rolls her eyes. "You don't know the half of it. Don't worry. I'll make sure Lemmy gets the works. Country omelet, bacon, and enough toast to sop up the sauce in his stomach."

I nod. "Thanks. Bring me another cup for some coffee, will ya?"

Sliding into the booth seat facing Lemmy, I lean back and give him a look. He's obediently conveying his steaming cup from the table to his mouth and back again. His eyes are unfocused, but when I say his name he does his best to look at me, squinting through his drunken haze.

"Zeb said you were causing a disturbance in the Lion's Tap, Lem. What's up with that?"

"Wasn't causin' no disturbance," he mumbles. "I'se just talkin', is all. Can't a guy talk anymore?"

"What about?"

"Can't remember…" he stares down into his cup. "Oh yeah! About how Zeb wouldn't serve me no more."

I let out a snort. "Is that all?"

"Yuh." He takes another gulp. "Is that any way to treat a reg'lar?"

Just then, Penny comes up with Lemmy's food, so I'm spared having to reply. Just as I'm pulling out my phone to text Gunner, it rings with an incoming call from Hawk.

"Where the fuck are you?" he barks without preamble. "I need you down here at the shop."

"Sorry. Something came up. Gunner needed me to pick up Lemmy."

At the sound of his name, Lemmy perks up and looks at me. I shake my head and point down at the food. *Eat.*

"Ah. Fuck. Okay," Hawk says grudgingly. "So, when you coming in?"

"Soon. I was just about to get hold of Gunner to find out when he's available to take over. He should be along as soon as he's done taking Alix to the doctor."

"Where you at?"

"Downtown Diner."

"Yeah?" Hawk's voice perks up. "Do me a favor and pick me up a burger and fries to go. I worked through lunch and I'm fuckin' starving."

"Doesn't that old lady of yours fix you lunch?" I tease him.

"Sam?" he laughs. "Sure, if I asked her to, she would. But I'm not into fuckin' salads. Or ants on a log, which is all Connor seems to want to eat right now."

"What the fuck? Ants on a log?" I briefly wonder if Hawk's lost his damn mind.

"Haven't you ever seen that shit? It's uh, celery with peanut butter in the middle, and raisins on top to look like ants sitting on it."

"That's fuckin' weird, man."

"Tell me about it. So yeah. Bring me a burger and fries. Extra ketchup."

"What am I, your servant?" I complain.

"Do it because you love me, brother. Gotta go."

Jesus. My brothers are all turning into a bunch of pussies with this family man garbage. I mean, don't get me wrong. I like Hawk's old lady Sam, and I'll admit his kid Connor is pretty cute. And I've never seen Gunner happier than when Alix is in the same room.

But Christ, I can practically feel my balls shriveling up, just being around all this happy family domestic shit. For fuck's sake, even Thorn's been talking about starting a family with his old lady, Isabel. *Thorn.*

I call over to Penny and tell her I need a burger and fries to go, extra ketchup. Then I sit in silence for a few minutes, watching as Lemmy devours his food like a starving man, which he probably is. I shoot Gunner a text letting him know where we are. A few seconds later, he texts back and says he should be here to pick Lemmy up by the time he's done with his food.

"I'll be in Alix's car," he writes.

Penny comes out with Hawk's order, which I pay for in cash. A few minutes later, just as Lem is finishing up his bacon, a late-model Kia pulls up next to my bike.

"Lemmy, your ride's here," I tell him.

Now that he's full of food he's pretty docile, and stands up without any prompting. "Can I take this with me?" he asks, holding up a piece of toast.

"Sure. Come on." I swing out of the booth, say goodbye to Penny, and guide him toward the door. At the last second, I realize I've left the to-go bag on the table. I wave Lemmy out the door and go back for it. Through the window, I see Gunner climb out of the car and lead his uncle toward the passenger side. I lift my chin in greeting at him. He gives me a wave.

I'm still looking back, watching Gun help Lemmy into the car, as I start to pull open the front door of the diner. There's resistance, so I pull harder, yanking on the handle.

A cry of alarm snaps me to attention. A chick with blond hair tumbles through the doorway. She pinwheels her arms forward in an attempt to regain her balance. In the process, she knock the to-go bag out of my hand and onto the floor, just before she falls right on top of it.

"Goddamn it!" I bark, more than anything pissed that I'm gonna have to order another burger for Hawk. "What the hell is wrong with —?"

And that's where my words fucking die in my throat. Because as she twists herself onto her butt and looks up at me, I catch a glimpse of a jawline, and then a nose, and there's something so unmistakably familiar about them both it's like a gut punch out of nowhere.

Fuck. Me.

It can't be. But it is.

Brooke fucking Brentano.

4
BROOKE

My God.

I was hoping against hope I could stay incognito when I was back in Tanner Springs.

I even entertained the fantasy that I could get through this entire thing without ever having to see a familiar face.

But even in my wildest, worst-case-scenario dreams, I couldn't have imagined the very first person I would run into — *literally run into* — would be someone I knew.

And even worse than that, it's the absolute *last* person from here I ever wanted to see again.

Travis Carr.

His name flashes immediately through my mind as I free-fall through the air and onto the plastic bag holding what must be a takeout order. I only saw his face for a millisecond before I bashed into him, but it was enough.

I'd know it anywhere. It's etched into my brain, more clearly than any other from my childhood.

I land hard on the bag, sprawling out like a starfish. I feel the Styrofoam inside collapse under me. The aroma of the food I've just smushed is unmistakable. *Hmmm… Burger and fries,* my brain registers. My stomach rumbles in agreement.

If I wasn't so mortified, I'd start laughing. But this is about as far from funny as it gets.

"Goddamn it!" Travis spits, clearly pissed that I've ruined his lunch. He can't have recognized me, I realize as I lie there on my stomach. His reaction is too normal. Absurdly, I wish I could just freeze time right at this second. Just close my eyes, stop everything right where it is, and disappear.

Then I wouldn't have to live through the next few seconds.

But of course, if I had those kinds of superpowers, a hell of a lot of things in my life would be different.

So instead, I take a deep breath, flip myself over onto my ass, and look up at him just as he's starting to demand what the hell is wrong with me.

When his eyes lock on my face, all the words die in his throat.

"Hello, Travis," I murmur.

He's never been an easy one to read. But all the same, I think I see half a dozen different emotions play across his features, all of them cycling and spinning like a roulette wheel.

I wonder which one he'll settle on.

I don't have long to wait.

"Well, ho-ly shit." Travis's upper lip curls into a lazy sneer. "Look what the cat dragged in." He shifts his gaze and nods toward the smashed burger and fries. "As per usual, you don't waste any time fucking other people's shit up, do you?"

I force down the angry, defensive retort that's leaping to my throat. *The quickest way to make this end is not to engage at all*, I tell myself.

"I'm sorry about that," I murmur. I put my arms underneath me and prepare to hoist myself up to my feet. He does *not* offer me a hand. "I'll pay for another order of that."

"Damn straight you will," he bites out, then calls out to a waitress standing in the back. "Hey Penny! Start me another order to go to replace the one this one here fucked up!"

Jesus. Okay, I always kind of assumed Travis would be mad at me for leaving town the way I did. I can't exactly blame him for that. But it's been quite a few years since then. Apparently, though, even after all this time, he's…

Still mad.

I look over at the waitress, who's eyeing the two of us with a curious expression. "Could you, um, give me the same thing, please?" I ask. "For here, though. And a Coke."

She hesitates for a second, then gives me a curt nod and disappears into the kitchen.

I'm standing now, feeling awkward as hell. I bend down to pick up the smashed bag and set it on the counter. "I'm sorry," I say to Travis again. Against my better judgment, I risk a glance up at his face.

The years have changed him considerably. To the point I'm almost surprised I recognized him. But it's definitely still *him.* His hair's still long — a shaggy, dark mane that frames his face down to his shoulders. His jaw is still square and handsome, with just enough of a beard to accentuate the masculine lines. His eyes are still that cool, intense shade of light blue. The color of a frozen lake.

The last time I saw him, there were traces of boyishness in his face, but that's completely gone. The person who looks back at me now is all man. He's grown a couple more inches in height since high school — he got to be at least six foot six now. And he's big — *huge*, actually. Hard and chiseled, and muscled enough for two men. Tattoos line his arms, drawing the eye to them. It's an effort not to stare at them all. He's wearing a simple black T-shirt, and a leather motorcycle club vest with patches that say *Lords of Carnage MC* and *Beast.*

He's in a biker club now.

Beast.

Huh. That must be his road name.

It fits.

I let out a soft snort, which Travis must take as a judgment because he narrows his eyes at me.

"You got a problem with this?" he asks, nodding down at his leather.

"Why should I?" I counter.

"Because you seem to have grown into a pretty straight arrow, sweetheart." His eyes slide up and down my frame mockingly. "What are you, some sort of real estate agent now?"

I suppose he's referring to my suit. And the no-nonsense below-the-chin haircut. It's not exactly the way I left here, to be sure. Back when Travis knew me, I looked a lot wilder. On the outside, anyway. Wavy blond hair that flowed in a mess down to my waist — more because I couldn't afford a haircut than from any conscious style choice. Flannel shirts, ripped jeans. Ill-fitting black boots. Dark eyeliner around my eyes, blood-red lipstick, and an overall, "Don't even fucking talk to me" attitude.

All that, to mask what was going on inside.

With most people, my fuck-off costume worked like a charm.

Travis had been one of the rare ones who managed to crack open the door to my soul that I kept shut so tightly.

A little wave of sadness for the girl I used to be rises up inside me, but I push it down.

"No." I shake my head. "I'm not a realtor."

I turn away from him and take a seat at one of the swivel stools lining the counter. I don't want to continue this conversation. And I'm sure he doesn't either. He's made it quite apparent that my presence here is unwelcome. I'll be doing both of us a favor if I give him an opportunity to stop talking to me.

I pull out my phone and pretend to check my email. But apparently, he's not done trying to get a rise out of me.

"Lawyer?" he guesses again. "One of those uptight corporate ones? Never figured you for a suit, B."

I don't bother replying.

"Quite the disappearing act you pulled," he drawls, a slight bitter edge to his voice. "What brings you back to lowly Tanner Springs? Felt like slumming it for a while?"

I don't know how to make him stop hounding me. I've been trained not to react or show any emotion under pressure. But even so, I find myself going on the defensive. "I didn't know you still cared that much!" I hiss, not bothering to turn around.

"I don't!" he fires back. "But you could have done everybody around here a favor and just stayed gone!"

"Believe me, I tried."

"So," he continues, sliding onto a seat two stools down from me. "Why the fuck *are* you back here, anyway?"

I audibly groan and roll my eyes. Turning to him, I open my mouth to answer. As I do, I see his gaze drift down to my chest. For a moment, I think he's staring at my breasts, and I almost call him on it. But then I see his eyes widen with a look of comprehension.

"Holy shit," he mutters, and I realize he's seen the outline of my gun, secure in its shoulder holster. "You're a *fed*." Disgust flickers across his face.

My mouth slams shut. I open it again to deny his words, but what's the point? He's perceptive, I'll give him that.

"Nice judgment," I fire back, looking pointedly at his cut. "I see *you've* fulfilled your role as a fine upstanding citizen."

"Fuck you."

I snort, happy in the knowledge that I scored a point in our sparring match. Feels good. *Fuck you too, Travis.*

I pointedly ignore him now, staring at my email as though it's of utmost importance, even though the only new messages I have are spammy ads for dating sites.

Which, seriously? How does the entire internet know I haven't had a date in almost four years?

A couple minutes later, our food comes. The waitress sets my plate down in front of me, and slides a plastic bag toward Travis. As I pull my plate toward me, Travis grabs his food.

"So, what's a spook like you doing in a shithole like this?" he growls. "Business or pleasure?"

I pick up my burger and take a bite. "Business. Not like it's any of yours."

I try to concentrate on eating, but Travis's baritone slides through the layers of my defenses. It's so familiar, so dark and velvety. His voice is deeper now, but the same resonance is still there. Like an echo, I can hear it in the chambers of my memory. Something buried down deep inside me — a long-banished emotion from the past — rises up to the surface, making my heart physically ache with a suddenness and acuteness that surprises me. Instinctively I bend over, as though to protect myself from the pain.

"How long are you planning to *grace* Tanner Springs with your presence?"

The harshness of Travis's tone snaps me back to reality.

"As little time as possible. Believe me," I half-whisper.

"*Good.*"

In spite of myself, the word cuts into me. It's not like I want him to be *glad* I'm back here. After all, if he *was* glad, he might try to see me again, which I *do not* want.

But I guess if I'm honest with myself, I'd prefer that he didn't *hate* me after all this time. Maybe he could have just been indifferent, or something.

Yeah, that's what I would have liked. Total indifference.

Because him hating me — having him right here, and *knowing* that he hates me — well, it hurts. It shouldn't, but it does. It makes me want to explain. Makes me want to justify myself. And I can't.

So I don't.

Instead, I pick up the bottle of ketchup sitting in front of me. I unscrew the cap, turn it upside down, and deliberately pour out a mound onto my plate. I screw the cap back on, take a fry, and drag it through the red before raising it to my mouth.

Travis waits a few seconds. Maybe he's expecting me to say something else. To give as good as I get.

When I don't, he turns on his heel and leaves without a word.

The bell on the front door of the diner announces his departure. I pick up my burger to take a bite, but set it down again as a sour feeling grows deep in the pit of my stomach. Suddenly, I'm not hungry at all.

5
BEAST

"Jesus fuck, Beast. What's crawled up your ass?"

Hawk's got half a burger in his hand as he stands over me, looking pissed. I've just managed to beat a ferocious dent in the side panel of a car I'm *supposed* to be restoring.

"Yeah, sorry about that," I mutter. "I got some shit on my mind."

"Well, get it *out* of your mind," he growls. "I ain't payin' you to create more work for me. Fuckin' A, you're supposed to be fixing that piece of shit, not destroying it."

"You know as well as I do that this car ain't worth a goddamn thing, restored or unrestored," I retort. The car in question is a rusted-out Mustang that our customer probably found in the back lot of his grandpa's farm or something. The condition it's in, it'd be better off as a hotel for raccoons. We're piecing it back together, and he wants it to look like new when were done. At this rate, there's more of it from junk yards than from the original car. I've taken to callin' it FrankenMustang.

"Yeah. I do. But Sam Weber's money is green just like everybody else's. And frankly, we need the green right now. So shut the hell up and fix your attitude. You're gonna punch a fist hole right through the rust."

Far from calming me down, Hawk's words just end up making me madder. I'm gonna end up beating the shit out of something — or someone — if I don't get out of here. I stand up and wipe my hands on my jeans. "I gotta take a break."

"Good. Come back when you're ready to play nice."

"Fuck you."

"Fuck you right back." Hawk shoots me a warning glare. I'm tempted to take a swing at him, but make myself back down. At six-foot seven, I'm easily the biggest member of the Lords of Carnage. But this is Hawk's shop. He's in charge here, and as much as he's pissing me off right now, I respect the way he runs the place. So instead of starting something, I flip him off and stomp outside for a smoke break.

Out in the back of the shop, there's plenty of shit for me to pound on. But instead of picking up a pipe and goin' to town, I sink down on an overturned five-gallon drum and light up. Taking a long drag, I blow the smoke noisily out of my lungs and try to get a grip on myself.

Fucking Brooke Brentano. *Fucking* Brooke Brentano.

I stand up abruptly from the five-gallon drum and start stomping through the yard. Ever since seeing her at the Downtown Diner, I can't get her out of my head. She looks totally different, but somehow still the same. She's all buttoned up now, with her uptight dark blue suit, tasteful makeup and not a hair out of place.

If anything, she's even more beautiful than she was at sixteen, even though I liked her better when she was wild, loose, and free. Her body is tighter now. More muscular. She has a tightly-coiled look, like she could spring into action and take down a man twice her size. Which I have no doubt she could do. Brooke was always a tough one. She didn't let a lot of people see past the fuck-you exterior, to what she was really like.

I was just starting to see inside her, when she left town. Left *me*.

With a roar, I drop my cigarette on the ground and pick up the fender of an old Buick, smashing it against the front windshield of a junker car. The glass shatters explosively.

The noise and destruction give me a moment's reprieve. But even as I pick my smoke back up from the dirt and put it back in my mouth, Brooke's face is back. My mind's eye roves over the curve of her jawline, down to the soft, vulnerable skin of her neck. The pressed fabric of her suit stops me momentarily, but I can still see the swell of her breasts, small and firm. My cock stirs as I imagine how they'd feel under my hands. I recall the creaminess of her skin, how soft it was. From the depths of my memory, I hear the faintest echo of the noise she made when I was giving her pleasure. I wonder if she would still make that noise.

My mind moves southward, sliding down her ribs toward her waist, when suddenly, it comes back to the outline of her gun, which snaps me back into reality.

She's a fuckin' fed.

Of all the things I could have imagined Brooke doing — of all the places I could have imagined she'd gone — being a federal agent is the absolute last thing I ever would have guessed. Shit, I could have seen her as, I dunno… a belly dancer? A singer in a rock band, maybe? Even a goddamn forest ranger. But a *fed*?

I pick up an old carburetor and throw it as hard as I can against the side window of the junker. That shatters, too.

Why do you even care what the fuck she is? a small, rational part of my brain argues. *It's not your fuckin' problem, Beast.* She *is not your fuckin' problem. And hasn't been for a long time.*

She was *never* my fuckin' problem, as it turned out. I was just too young, dumb, and full of come to know it at the time.

I never really knew her anyway, did I? I was just an idiot kid. I didn't know what the hell I wanted. Brooke was just the first piece of tail who seemed like she had a brain rattling around in there somewhere. I let my dick do my thinking for me. It was all just a stupid mistake.

And now she's back in town. For who knows how long. To make my life goddamn miserable, unless I can stay the hell away from her. Unless I can stop my dick from thinking, and use my big head instead of my little head where she's concerned, for once.

Fuck.

I finish my smoke, and shrug off my cut. Then I grab a tire iron and start wailing on a pile of old tires by the side of the lot. Over and over, I bring the metal down, as hard as I can, feeling my muscles strain and flex with the effort. I keep pounding until I'm exhausted, dripping with sweat and my mind almost clear.

"Hey!"

I turn around. Hawk is standing about twenty feet behind me. His arms are crossed, and he's surveying the scene in front of him.

"God damnit, Hawk, do *not* fuckin' break my balls right now!" I growl. "I'll fuckin' pay for whatever you think this junk is worth." I drop the tire iron and pull my shirt off over my head, using it to wipe the sweat off my face and chest.

"Fuck that. All this shit's just goin' to the junk yard." Hawk replies easily. "Besides, it looks like you need to let off some steam. Wanna talk about it?"

"What are you, my therapist?" I bark. "No, I do not want to fucking *talk about it.* Jesus!"

Hawk shrugs. "Suit yourself." The hint of a smirk ghosts across his face. Smug fucker.

"So, if you ain't out here to bitch at me, what the fuck do you want?" I challenge.

Hawk's smirk disappears.

"I just got a call from Trudy," he says, a frown creasing his brow. "She's at the hospital. Rock's been admitted for a heart attack."

* * *

"Jesus," I mutter to myself under the sound of my engine. "What the fuck is *up* with this day?" It seems destined to throw me one goddamn curve ball after another. I'm lookin' forward to drowning my sorrows in the bottom of a bottle of Jack when this is over.

We're riding in formation to Tanner Springs General Hospital. Since Rock, our prez, isn't with us, our VP Angel is in his spot, in front and to the left. Normally Gunner, our Road Captain, would be riding beside him, but Gun is still off dealing with Lemmy and he's not back yet. So instead Geno, our Secretary/Treasurer, is filling that spot. I'm further back, just in front of Ghost, our Sergeant at Arms.

I don't know much more about Rock's situation, except that he's awake, and out of danger for the moment.

When we get to the hospital, we park in a group at the top of the parking garage, then take the elevator down to the floor that says it houses the cardiac unit. On the way in, I notice the black BMW SUV belonging to Rock's old lady, parked in a spot near the door. I know it's hers because of the vanity plate:

BACKOFF

At the info desk, Angel asks a gray-haired lady with a thin, chinless face where Rock Anthony's room is. She casts furtive glances around at the group of us as she slowly pecks his name into the computer. For a moment, she looks like she's having second thoughts about giving us the number, but finally purses her lips and murmurs it to Angel.

"Thanks," he says, and lifts his chin at the rest of us to follow.

Most of us aren't talking much. It's a somber thing when your club president is out of commission, even if it's only temporary. When we get to the corridor where they're keeping Rock, I see Trudy coming out of a door on the right-hand side. As usual, she's got her dyed-blond hair teased up into a high pony on top of her head. She's wearing a tailored black leather jacket and tight dark jeans that hug her ample figure, and swaying a little on her high black boots. When she sees us coming down the hall, she turns and starts walking toward us.

"Tru." Angel steps forward, and she allows herself to be embraced.

"Angel." She's taken out a pack of cigarettes, which she holds nervously in her red-lacquered hands.

"How is he?"

Trudy raises an eyebrow. "He's about how you'd expect him to be. Weak. Tired. Acting like an asshole to the docs."

Angel snorts. "Yeah. About the size of it."

Geno cuts in. "What happened? Were you with him when it went down?"

Trudy's jaw tenses. Something in her face shifts. "No. I was not," she says coldly. "The hospital called me after they brought him in."

Next to me, Ghost, lets out a low whistle that only I can hear. Something's up.

"Now that you're all here," Trudy continues, her eyes sweeping over us, "I'm going out for a smoke and a coffee. I'll be back in a little while. You make sure that old fool doesn't do anything stupid while I'm gone."

"Sure thing, Tru," Angel reassures her. Trudy's heels clack down the hall as she walks past us, head high, and goes in the direction of the elevators.

"Wonder what Rock's done to get the cold shoulder?" Ghost murmurs.

"Wonder if is has anything to do with what he was doing when he had the attack," I mutter back. Trudy and Rock have always had a bit of a tempestuous relationship, but I've never known anything to be seriously wrong between them. She and Rock have been together a long time. She knows what being the old lady of an MC prez is about.

There's too many of us for everyone to go into Rock's room at once, so five of us head in first while the rest wait outside. Angel, Ghost, Geno, Thorn and I slip inside the open door of Rock's private room, pushing aside the privacy curtain so we can all fit at once.

"Oh, Jesus, look at this. It's the welcome wagon," Rock grouses as he sees us walk in.

"Go ahead and complain, old man," Thorn shoots back, flashing him a teasing grin. "A cranky cunt like you'd be lucky to have this many people show up for your funeral."

Far from being insulted, Rock finds Thorn's remark amusing. He starts laughing, his head rising up off the pillow, but then the laughter turns to a cough and he falls back on the bed, clutching weakly at the sheets.

"Don't fuckin' do that," he finally manages to wheeze.

"Sorry, prez," Thorn mutters.

"So, how you feelin', Rock?" Ghost asks.

"Like shit. How you think I'm feelin'?" He lifts up an arm to show us the IV drip plugged into him. "Look at all this bullshit," he says in disgust. "I can't wait to get out of here."

"When *are* you gonna get out?" Angel asks. "The docs say anything?"

"Nah, not yet. They're keepin' me here overnight for sure. Beyond that, what the fuck do I know? They keep sayin' they gotta keep me here for observation. Make sure they know the extent of the damage to my ticker." He shakes his head and grumbles. "They say maybe I gotta change my diet, start takin' pills or somethin'. Fuck that."

"Who brought you in, Rock?" I ask.

"I brought *myself* in!" he barks back. "Okay?"

"Christ, okay," I raise a hand. "Just wonderin' what you were doin' when it happened. Were you exerting yourself, or somethin'?"

"Jesus fuck! None of your goddamn business, okay?" he splutters. "Christ, if I'd known I was gonna get the third degree, I wouldn'ta let any of you fuckers in here. You're all worse than goddamn Trudy."

Behind us, the door pushes open and a familiar figure in a nurse's uniform comes in.

"Well, hello there," Thorn's old lady Isabel says. She just recently completed nursing school and was lucky enough to land a job here at Tanner Springs General. She looks around the room at all of us and flashes Thorn a quick smile.

"How are you feeling, Rock?"

"Does everybody gotta ask me that question?" he answers irritably.

"The nurses and doctors do," she smiles, pretending to ignore his rudeness. "Otherwise, how are we going to know how to take care of you?"

"I don't need anyone to take care of me," Rock grumps.

Isabel rolls her eyes and grins. "This is a lot of people to be visiting our patient," she points out. "You guys look like clowns trying to fit into a Volkswagen in here."

"Yeah, get 'em outta here," Rock echoes. He raises a hand and waves us off.

Thorn takes a step forward and catches his old lady around the waist. "Hey, there, gorgeous," he growls. "Ya know, I'm not feelin' that great meself. What's a man gotta do to get some nursing around here?"

Isabel giggles and flashes him a radiant smile. "Don't you get enough of that at home, sir?"

"Ah, geez, enough of that," Rock grunts, but Isabel's presence seems to have lightened the mood just a little.

"All right," Angel says. "We'll get out and let the next group come in to say hello."

"Angel," Rock says suddenly. "The shipment tomorrow." He glances at Isabel, but then keeps talking. "I won't be there to lead the run. You gotta make sure things go through."

"Don't worry, Rock. It's handled." Angel claps him gently on the shoulder. "You got nothing to worry about. Everything's under control until you get outta here. Okay?"

"Yeah. Okay." Rock leans his head back on the pillow and closes his eyes.

The five of us file out of the room. Isabel comes out with us.

"I know he looks like hell right now," she tells us. "But actually, his vitals look okay. The heart attack could have been a lot worse. It was a warning. Hopefully, a wake-up call. If he takes it seriously, and changes a few things in his lifestyle, there's every reason to believe he'll come out of this just fine."

Ghost smirks. "Hard to imagine Rock eatin' a low sodium diet and drinking green tea." That gets a chuckle out of the rest of us.

Angel tells the rest of the brothers that the five of us are gonna take off back to the clubhouse. On the way out, I half-expect to run into Trudy, but she's nowhere in sight. Back out in the parking garage, I see why: her car's gone.

"Looks like Trudy's taken off for a while," I say to Angel, pointing to the empty space.

"Huh." Angel doesn't seem surprised. I lift a brow at him.

"She seemed pretty mad at him," I remark.

"Well, that might be because of this, or it might just be in general," Angel answers reluctantly. "Trudy and Rock are on the rocks."

"Yeah?"

"Yeah. She kicked him out of the house a couple weeks ago. He's been sleeping at the club. Apparently, she wants a divorce."

6
BROOKE

After I manage to choke down half a burger and a few fries, I pay the waitress at the diner for my meal and Travis's, then head over to the hotel to check in.

I'm still trying to convince myself that running into him like this was a *good* thing. Good that it happened right away, I mean. And especially good that he's mad at me. That means he'll avoid me from now on, and I can just focus on my work.

Work. That's what comes next. I need to clear everything else from my mind.

I walk into the lobby of the chain hotel on the edge of town where I booked my reservation. The place is brand-spanking new, so much so that the furniture in the lobby still has that weird off-gassing smell to it. I approach the front desk, rolling my suitcase behind me. A young girl who can't be more than nineteen greets me with an overly-lipsticked smile. From the name tag pinned to her shirt, I gather her name is Brandi.

"Hi. I have a reservation under Brentano."

The girl nods, a parody of adult efficiency, and reaches down to pick up the single paper lying on the counter in front of her. "Absolutely," she enthuses. "Brentano, single occupancy? Looks like you'll be with us for… three days?"

"That's right." I watch as she turns to a monitor and starts to clack at the keys with multicolored nails. "I may have to extend my stay at some point," I continue. "Will that be a problem?" It seems like a ridiculous question, given that there are only four cars in the whole parking lot, but I figure I should ask.

"I'm sure it should be fine," she smiles politely. "Just let us know as soon as you're able to. Worst case scenario, we'd just have to have you switch rooms. Would that be okay?"

I shrug, even though I can't imagine why that would be necessary. "Sure."

Brandi types some more information into the computer, frowning in concentration. She asks for my credit card, which I provide, and then clacks some more. Finally, she reaches for a tiny envelope. "One room key fine?"

"That'll do it."

"Okay!" she says chirpily. She scrawls a number on the envelope, slips a card in, and hands it to me. "Your room number is here," she says, pointing with a colored nail. "Elevators are down the hall and to the left. You'll be on the fourth floor. Please let us know if you need anything."

"I will. Thanks." I take the card from her and turn down the hall, happy to be done with the transaction. I don't know why, but I've always found these kinds of conversations exhausting and unpleasant. It's not quite fair — Brandi's just doing her job, after all. I just kind of hate the whole official-speak of it. It makes me feel like we're all robots, instead of human beings.

As the elevator takes me up to my room on the top floor of the hotel, I shrug it off and turn my mind to the rest of the afternoon. My first order of business is to stop in and see the chief of the Tanner Springs Police Department. A Brandt Crup, apparently. I don't recognize the name, so I'm guessing he's not from Tanner Springs originally — meaning he probably won't recognize or know anything about me, which is a plus. I called yesterday and spoke to his assistant, who told me she'd convey the message that I'd be stopping by sometime today.

Sliding my key card through the slot, I enter the room, turn on the light, and glance around at my new home for the next few days. Nothing glamorous, but more than adequate. I take off my jacket and remove my shoulder holster, then bend down and do a few stretches to work the kinks out of my neck and shoulders. I toss my bag on one of the two beds and decide to spend a few minutes checking my emails, which yields nothing important. Resisting the urge to lie down on the other bed, I instead go into the bathroom to splash some water on my face. A minute later, I'm strapping my holster back on, complete with the familiar weight of the .40 caliber Smith & Wesson that FBI agents carry.

Travis noticed my gun almost immediately.

In my mind's eye, I see his look of disgust. His curled lip.

We sure did end up on opposite sides of the law. Though to be honest, anyone who was guessing about our futures ten years ago probably would be more surprised by my career choice than his.

I see his deep, cool eyes, staring right through me. Those eyes, that used to know me so well.

And at the same time, that didn't know me at all.

* * *

I pull my jacket back on and make sure it's buttoned and that the holster is concealed. Then I head back out to my car to make the journey to the Tanner Springs Police Department.

One thing about Tanner Springs: it doesn't take very long to get anywhere. I'm parked and walking up to the building within ten minutes. I remembered the location from when I lived here as a kid. The squat, sprawling brick structure with its angular green roof brings back uncomfortable memories.

But as with every memory about Tanner Springs, I stuff them down inside me.

A guard behind Plexiglass directs me to where I need to go, and soon I find myself standing at a large desk where a small, efficient-looking woman is sitting. The name plate in front of her tells me her name is Joyce.

"Hello," I say, pulling out a card and handing it to her. "I'm Agent Brooke Brentano. I called earlier. I'm here to see Chief Crup."

The woman looks up at me and takes the card I offered. She stares down at it. "From the FBI?" she asks, her eyes widening. She looks at me like she doesn't quite know what to make of me.

"Yes, that's right. Is Chief Crup in?"

"He, ah…" she glances back toward a closed door which must lead to his office. I get the distinct feeling she doesn't want to disturb him, but she doesn't quite dare turn me down. "Yes, just one moment."

Joyce gets out of her chair and goes to the door. She taps on it a couple of times and then turns the knob softly. I see her hunch a little, almost apologetically, as she enters.

I wait there, taking in my surroundings. The office is a large, open area, with quite a few desks distributed around the room. Uniformed officers of different ages talk on the phone or work on computers. A couple of them look up at me curiously.

I notice that of the dozen or so people here, Joyce is the only woman.

"Chief Crup will see you now," Joyce murmurs, coming back outside. She's no longer carrying my card, so I'm assuming she gave it to him.

"Thank you," I smile.

"Oh, would you like some coffee?" she asks, flustered, as though she's remembering her manners.

"I'm fine," I reassure her. Joyce steps back, letting me pass, and I push open the door to the chief's office.

Chief Brandt Crup stands up to greet me. He's holding my card in his left hand as he reaches out his right to shake mine. He's a fairly nondescript man, medium build. I'd place him somewhere in his early forties. He's got a bit of a paunch, which causes the buttons on his blue shirt to pull ever-so-slightly.

"Agent… Brentano," he greets me, glancing at my card. His face is expressionless. "What can I do for you?"

The first thing that strikes me about him is his overly officious air — an attitude that is enhanced by the multiple framed pictures on his wall shaking hands and smiling with various men in suits. *Pillar of the community,* I muse to myself ironically.

"I'm sorry to show up more or less unannounced, Chief Crup," I begin. Normally, I don't apologize when I'm working — for *anything*. As a female FBI agent, I'm already operating at a disadvantage by people who don't take me as seriously as they would a male agent. But there's something about this man that makes me instinctively decide to proceed carefully. His rigid posture tells me he's already on his guard. By softening — feminizing — my approach, I'm hoping to get him to relax that a little.

"Not at all," he replies magnanimously, motioning for me to sit down. His shoulders loosen just a hair. *Bingo.*

"I'm here from the Cleveland field office," I continue, sliding into a seat opposite him. "I've been assigned to follow up on a call we got from a citizen in your community."

"What sort of call?" He leans back in his chair and gives me an indulgent smirk.

This is where it gets tricky. I'm under no obligation to give Chief Crup any information. In fact, there's nothing saying I even need to have this conversation at all. FBI agents are not required to work with, or even inform, local law enforcement of their comings and goings. Often, they don't.

But I know Tanner Springs — at least, I used to. A small town like this, it doesn't take long before people notice a stranger walking around, and start asking questions. I made a calculated decision to tell the PD I'm here, before someone sees me sniffing around and calls them.

"I'm not at liberty to say," I reply, stepping carefully. "It's very possibly a false tip. But the agency has a duty to follow up on it anyway. I'm just letting you know I'll be here in town for a few days."

Chief Crup's eyes narrow, just a hair. It's clear he doesn't like the fact that I'm keeping him in the dark.

"If you let us know what's going on, I could assign an officer to you," he suggests, peering at me. "Help you out, show you around town."

I don't offer that I'm not a stranger to Tanner Springs. "Thank you, but that won't be necessary."

Crup is not impressed with my answer. "Where'd you say you're from? Which field office?"

"Cleveland."

"Little lady," he begins, leaning forward. He puts his elbows on the desk, and fists one hand into the other below his chin. "I'm sure Tanner Springs sure ain't Cleveland. But you might find you'll want some backup with you when you go around confronting strangers." He gives me an indulgent smile. "People here don't always take kindly to outsiders. You take one of my men along with you, the citizens of our fair city might be a lot more likely to talk to you."

And you'll be able to keep an eye on me, I think.

In my experience, local PDs run the gamut from cooperative, to indifferent, to hostile when confronted with the FBI entering their turf.

Looks like this one's gonna be hostile.

And sexist, to boot.

It's probably just that he's one of those guys with some sort of superiority complex. He likes being in charge. Likes the people around them to take a deferential attitude.

Still, there's something going off inside my head as I stare at him. A tiny alarm bell, sounding somewhere in the far-off reaches of my brain.

I tamp down the urge to knock him down a peg or two, and try to see the situation from my advantage. Since I'm a younger woman, it's possible he'll just dismiss me as incompetent or unimportant. And then he'll leave me alone.

"I can handle myself, thank you, Chief."

His smile fades a little. "Well," he says dubiously, "suit yourself. But let me know if you change your mind." He stands up, clearly indicating we're done here. "How long did you say you'll be in town?"

"Not long. A few days, probably."

"Anything I should know? Anything you're *at liberty* to tell me?" he asks, his tone slightly mocking.

"Not at the moment. I'll be in touch if that changes."

I leave Chief Crup's office, feeling unsettled without quite knowing why. To be honest, this is about how I would have expected our conversation to go. But still. Something tells me if I don't treat the chief of the Tanner Springs PD with kid gloves, I might have more interference from him and his men than I bargained for.

7
BEAST

Huh. Trudy and Rock are on the outs.

Now that Angel mentions it, I guess Rock has been sleeping at the club a lot lately. It's not unusual for him to stay in his apartment in the clubhouse. Especially if we party into the night, or if one of the club girls catches his eye that evening. I never noticed he was there every night, though.

Not that it's any of my fuckin' business. But I like Trudy, even though she's kind of rough around the edges. For her to be mad at Rock, he must have fucked up big-time with her. Hell, for as long as I've known her, she's always taken the club stuff in stride. She's the old lady of an MC prez, after all. She knows Rock is no saint. Shit, she even knows he's been fucking our club girl Tammy on the regular for a while. But Trudy's always looked the other way at Rock's indiscretions.

I don't ask Angel anything else about the situation, though. As long as shit continues as usual in the club, I keep my nose out of everyone else's private life.

"I'm gonna call church when we get back to the clubhouse," Angel tells me as we climb onto our bikes. "I need to make sure everyone knows about Rock. And since he ain't gonna be going on the run with us tomorrow, I need to make sure everyone's on the same page about how it's gonna go down."

"Understood." I was planning on stopping at home after this, but instead I follow Angel's lead out of the hospital ramp and ride with the others back to the clubhouse. When we get there, I head immediately to the bar and ask Jewel to grab me a beer and pour me a shot of whiskey.

"Long day?" she asks with a smile as she reaches into the cooler.

"Holy shit, yes," I mutter. She takes the cap off the beer and sets it in front of me, then pours some amber-colored liquid into a shot glass.

"You may as well leave the bottle," I tell her. "I'm gonna want a couple of these."

"You got it." Jewel sets the whiskey down next to my beer and moves down the bar to grab a drink for someone else.

"Hey, brother." Gunner's voice behind me makes me turn around. Eyeing the whiskey bottle, he reaches across the counter and grabs a shot glass for himself. "Looks like you got the right idea."

"You got that right." I watch as he pours himself a drink. "How'd things go with Lemmy?"

Gunner grimaces. "Oh, fuck. I managed to get him back home. He's sleepin' it off. At least, I hope he's still asleep." He slams the whiskey back and sets the shot glass on the counter. "Thanks for helpin' me out with him."

"No worries. How was Alix's appointment with the doc?"

At this change in subject, Gunner breaks into a broad grin. "Good. Doc says she's about ready to pop." He laughs. "Well, he didn't exactly say it that way. But everything's lookin' good. Baby's pointing in the right direction. The doc measured a bunch of shit I didn't follow, but apparently that's good too."

"How's Alix doing?"

"Tired. Cranky. Has to pee all the time. Says she feels as big as a planet. But she's doing great. I think she's mostly looking forward to not being pregnant anymore. She wants to move on to the bein' a mom thing."

"How about you?"

"I'm not gonna lie, I'm kinda ready for it to be over, too." Gunner grabs another shot. "I'm lookin' forward to meetin' the little bugger. And I wouldn't mind gettin' back to normal in the bedroom. The last few weeks Alix has been too scared to have sex, afraid we'll hurt the baby. A man can only have so many blow jobs."

I crack up. "First world problems, brother. First world problems."

He starts laughing, too. "Yeah. They are pretty great blow jobs, too."

Down at the other end, Lug Nut is causing a scene trying to do some sort of weird plank thing off the side of the bar. Gunner catches me staring and snorts. "Eden's been challenging him to do yoga."

Eden is Alix's sister, and Lug Nut's woman. She's a recovered heroin addict. The club rescued her from a bunch of men who were trying to move her into prostitution. That's how Alix and Gunner met. Gunner's ma is the one who helped Eden detox and turn her life around. These days, Eden's a yoga instructor at one of the local foofy health clubs.

"Lug, what the fuck are you doing?" I yell. "You look like an asshole!"

"What? Yoga's fuckin' hard!" Lug protests. "Eden can do this shit for longer than any of you fuckers can."

"Okay, Yogi," Angel calls out from across the room. "Show and tell time's over. And the rest of you, listen up. Church in five!"

"Jewel!" I lift a finger at her. "I'll take a beer for the road."

"Two," Gunner adds.

"Coming right up, gentlemen."

I take a second to appreciate our bartender's fine ass as she bends over to grab us two more bottles. *Damn.*

"Have a good meeting," she replies as she sets them in front of us.

I reach into my pocket and pull out a five-dollar bill, which I stuff into her tip jar. "Thanks, darlin'," I nod. Turning to Gunner, I ask, "Shall we?"

He drains his last shot and slams the glass on the counter. "Leave the bottle there, honey," he says to Jewel. "We'll be back."

* * *

"So, Rock's gonna be laid up for a week or two. Maybe more," Angel is saying. "Meantime, any problems or issues with the club, you come to me. Understood?"

A murmur of assent is his response. "We still meeting up with the Outlaw Sons tomorrow?" Tank asks.

"Yeah. No change on that. We go ahead as planned." Angel's jaw is set, his brow tense. The Outlaw Sons isn't a club we've done business with before. They're a club to the north of us, and there's been some bad blood between us in the past. The Sons used to have a business partnership with a club we were at war with, called the Iron Spiders. We didn't know what kind of product they moved back and forth between them — only that the partnership existed. Little by little, the war between the Spiders and our club heated up, and eventually exploded. In the end, the Lords of Carnage destroyed the Iron Spiders' clubhouse and decimated their leadership. We ended their president, and all their officers. Since then, there's been no trace of the Spiders in the area.

A few weeks ago, Dragon, the president of the Outlaw Sons, approached Rock with a proposal to do business moving gun shipments with the Lords. Our club had gotten mostly out of gun running, until pretty recently when we struck up a deal with a club to our east, the Death Devils. We've been running for them for a little while now, and not looking to expand. But after talking to the prez of the Sons, Rock came back to the club and told us the terms they were offering were too good to refuse.

Truth be told, the money in guns is always good, and less of a hassle than drugs for the most part. Our territory is directly to the south of the Outlaw Sons, so it stands to reason they want an open channel going through us. And apparently they're willing to pay big for our cooperation.

"They want us to run the guns for them, or just safe passage?" Hawk asks.

"Little of both, dependin' on what we say about it."

"If we're runnin' the guns through territory ourselves, we need to worry about keeping the law off our backs," Ghost remarks. "Hope they're willing to make it worth our time."

"Rock's been talking to their prez some more about it. Tomorrow's supposed to be a first face to face meeting, to hear them out, but Rock's already given them what he considers our terms. I'm gonna go back to the hospital after this and talk to him some more. See what he's said to 'em already. Find out if there's anything we should be prepared for."

Thorn nods. "Good plan."

"What time we meetin' here tomorrow?" Sarge asks.

Angel snorts. "You wantin' to know how fucked up you can get tonight and still have time to sleep it off?"

Sarge grins. "Might be."

Angel lifts his chin and looks around the table. "Be here by late morning. We take off from here at noon."

He bangs the gavel. The men stand. Someone opens the door to the chapel.

"Let's get back to that whiskey," Gunner suggests.

"What if Alix goes into labor while you're here drinkin' with us?"

"She's with Eden. The two of them are goin' out for Mexican tonight. Besides, the doc said it'll be at least a few weeks yet. I'll get one of the prospects to hang around and stay sober just in case." He claps an arm around my shoulder. "C'mon, brother. We got a bottle to finish."

Never one to turn down an offer to drink with one of my brothers, I follow Gunner back to our seats at the bar, where Jewel has set out two clean shot glasses for us. The rest of the night is a raucous blur of music, laughter, and a couple of drunken fights.

By the time I stumble up to my apartment with one of the club girls in tow, I've managed to put both Rock's heart attack and Brooke goddamn Brentano's reappearance in Tanner Springs *way* the fuck out of my mind.

8
BROOKE

It's Friday, so I place a call to my boss before he takes off for the day. I phone the line to his office, and get put on hold for the better part of five minutes. Finally, the line clicks and Special Agent Lafontaine's voice comes over the line.

"Lafontaine."

"It's Agent Brentano, sir. I'm in Tanner Springs. Just checking in."

"Fine." He sounds brusque and a little annoyed.

"I've liaised with the chief of police here, Crup. On my way to talk to the source of the tip now."

"The police chief tell you anything useful?"

"No. He was a little less than welcoming."

"Well," Lafontaine replies with exaggerated patience, "You'll just have to deal with that."

It feels as though he's talking to a child. My blood starts to heat up, but I don't rise to the bait.

"I'll do some rooting around over the weekend and contact you Monday with an update."

"Don't feel there's any need to keep in such constant contact unless you have anything real to report, Brentano." He says in a clipped voice.

"Yes, sir."

"Is that all?"

"Yes, sir."

"All right."

The line goes dead. A sound of suppressed fury rises up in my throat. I hold up the phone and stick my tongue out at it — then hate myself for being the child that Lafontaine was treating me like.

"God —!" I begin to swear, then shake my head and snort in disgust. What the fuck is up his ass? I'm sick of his bullshit. I'm a goddamn FBI agent.

And I feel like the errand girl who's been sent out for an order of coffee that nobody wants.

Speaking of coffee, I'm in the mood for some, if only to have something to give me a little mood boost. I spotted a little shop on Main Street in downtown earlier that looks promising, so I head in that direction. I park my car in front of the shop, which is called The Golden Cup, and treat myself to a medium skim latte to go. The woman behind the counter who serves me is an attractive redhead about my age, pleasant and efficient. The coffee ends up being delicious, too. My mood has improved slightly by the time I push out the door with my cup and get back in my car.

The map app on my phone takes me to the address of the business whose owner filed the tip I'm here to check out. It ends up being in an aging strip mall, on the opposite side of town from my hotel.

As I'm parking, I happen to glance in my rear view mirror. I catch a glimpse the logo of what I think is the Tanner Springs PD on the side panel of a car. Shifting in my seat, I peer through the back window just in time to notice a police car driving slowly past the mini-mall.

Huh. Looks like I've got a babysitter.

Of course, it could just be a coincidence. But in my line of work, I've learned that coincidences are few and far between. It looks like Chief Crup has assigned someone to keep an eye on my comings and goings.

I wait until the cop car vanishes down the street. Then I push open my door and step out into the afternoon sun, taking my coffee with me. The sandwich shop I'm looking for is on one end of this mini-mall. The laundromat the business owner called us about is at the other end. I vaguely recall this mall from when I was younger. If I remember correctly, there used to be a video store here, and a nail salon, and a pet shop. Now, about a third of the businesses appear to be empty. Besides the sub shop, there's an insurance place, and one of those twenty-four hour gyms. My car is one of the only ones in the lot.

I step into the sub shop. The front of the store is deserted, but the sound of the bell must alert someone because I hear footsteps coming toward me from the back. A second later, a small, dark man with tufts of dark hair on either side of his balding pate comes up to the counter.

"Can I help you?"

"Mr. Pavel?"

"Yes?" He arches a brow at me.

I hand him my card. "I'm Agent Brentano. FBI. I'm following up on a tip you submitted using our online form."

Mr. Pavel takes the card from me and scrutinizes it, then pulls his eyes back to my face. "You're from the FBI?" he asks, looking less than convinced.

"Yes. I'm from the field office in Cleveland, Mr. Pavel. Do you have a few minutes to talk?"

He sweeps the hand holding my card around the deserted shop. "I'm doing nothing else," he says with a tinge of irony.

We sit down at one of the empty plastic booths near the window. "Can you tell me what led you to submit this tip, Mr. Pavel?" I ask, setting my coffee in front of me.

"Haven't you read it?"

"Yes," I explain patiently. "But I'd like to hear you tell me everything in person."

"It's the laundry business over there," he says, pointing. "E-Z Wash Express."

"What about it?"

"I think it's a front. For prostitution. Sex slaves!" He raises his bushy brows at me, dropping his voice conspiratorially.

He seems almost gleeful about this, despite the fact that he's *tsk*'ing and shaking his head. For a moment I feel like an idiot. Is this just some crank conspiracy wacko who sees criminal activity around every corner?

"You're speaking of human trafficking, Mr. Pavel," I say, keeping my voice carefully neutral. "Can you tell me what leads you to believe that this laundromat could be involved in something like that?"

"I go into the laundromat. To see what is happening. Whether there are people there. There are so many open washers and dryers!" Mr. Pavel grows animated, his hands beginning to wave in the air. "Why so many open washers and dryers? Almost no one doing laundry!"

"Isn't it possible that the laundry just isn't doing very good business?" I glance outside and nod toward the rest of the mall. "It seems like this place has seen better days."

"But that is just it! There are constantly people coming and going, coming and going! Men! So many men! And then sometimes, young girls. Why would middle-aged men in suits go into a laundromat?"

"Isn't that a little sexist, Mr. Pavel?" I ask. "Men have dirty laundry, too. Maybe they're divorced," I suggest. "Maybe they're estranged from their wives and living in apartments without a laundry facility."

"Why would they come without bags of laundry then?"

"Wait." I cock my head at him, puzzled. "You're saying that the people who are coming and going from the laundry aren't actually carrying bags of laundry?"

"Yes!" Mr. Pavel nods his head emphatically up and down. "No laundry! And they stay, for an hour, but if you go inside, they are not there. Then they come out, get in their cars, drive away. No laundry. No nothing."

Huh. This actually might be something after all. It's not a lot. In fact, it's hardly anything. But it is at least enough to merit a follow-up.

"Mr. Pavel. Can you tell me why you decided to report this to the FBI, instead of going to your police department?"

He wrinkles his nose in disgust. "I tried to talk to police. They told me I was just jealous that the laundromat gets more business than I do." He locks eyes with me. "So I contact you."

I sit for a moment, considering. "Is there anything else you can tell me? Do you know the owners? Have you ever talked to them?"

"No, I do not know the owner. There is a woman who works there. Now when she sees me, she tells me to leave." His eyes furrow. "She does not like me asking questions. She thinks I'm a crazy old man."

I take a deep breath and let it out. "Okay. Thank you for your time, Mr. Pavel. And your information."

"I am not a crazy old man," he insists.

"I'm sure you aren't," I say, giving him a neutral smile. "By the way, before I go, can I order one of your turkey subs?" I ask, glancing at the menu. I may as well grab something for dinner to stow in my mini-fridge while I'm here.

Mr. Pavel is delighted to make me a sandwich. While I'm waiting, I stare out the window and watch the traffic go by. No one drives into or out of the parking lot.

My turkey sub ready, I pay with a card and put a dollar in his tip jar. I tell Mr. Pavel goodbye and thank him for his time. Out at my car, I set the sandwich and my now-empty coffee cup inside, then lock it and walk over to the other side of the mall.

There are a couple of cars parked in the spaces in front of the laundromat, which is next to a tiny hole-in-the-wall pizza joint that looks permanently closed. But strangely, the laundromat is dark inside. A plastic sign hanging in the window is flipped to the "closed" side. I try the door, but it's locked. Frowning, I rap on the glass a few times. No response. Then I notice the business hours posted under the sign.

On Fridays, this place is supposed to be open until nine in the evening.

I knock on the glass again, but I don't really expect an answer. I wish I'd happened to notice when I drove in whether the laundromat was open then. Turning away from the door, I take a quick note of the make and model of the two cars sitting in front, just in case. I grab a small pad of paper from my blazer pocket and write down the license plate numbers of both cars. Then I wander down the row of shops, looking into each one to see if there are any customers. There's no one in the insurance place but a lone employee staring at a computer screen. In the fitness place next door, a couple of people are working out on some machines. I go inside and ask each of them whether either of the cars in front of the laundromat is theirs. Both of them say no.

Hmm.

Well, at the very least, this deserves another visit back to the laundromat when it's open. I walk back to my car, and point it in the direction of my hotel on the other side of town.

I drive back, my mind turning over everything I've just seen.

On the way, another cop car — an SUV this time — pulls in behind me, about half a block back. He stays with me until I turn into the hotel parking lot, then continues down the road.

The girl is roused from sleep, bruised and broken.

The men and the older woman are yelling at her. They're speaking so fast that the girl doesn't understand many of the English words. Only "cunt" and "go" and "now."

She and the other girls rise from their mattresses. The men shout some more, and the girls who know English start to get dressed and pull their few possessions together. She does the same, her heart hammering in her chest. One of the men comes up to her, mimes her picking up her thin mattress and blanket. She does, and hoists it over her thin shoulders like the others do.

They stumble up the stairs, in a groggy line. Past the rooms where during the day the men come to fuck them. Only a naked bulb lights their way. The girl almost falls once, but catches herself, afraid she'll be beaten if she slows down.

Outside, she is surprised to see the nighttime. She hasn't seen the sun or the moon in so long. This moon is clear. It is beautiful. So beautiful it makes her throat close, and tears well up. It has been so long since she has seen it, a moon this full. The last time was across the world. A lifetime ago.

They are shoved into a truck, one practically on top of the other. She finds Katya, the other girl from home.

"Where are they taking us?" she whispers.

"I don't know." Katya's eyes glow wide in the moonlight. "I heard one of the men say they had to hurry. Maybe they have to move us. Maybe someone found out. The police."

A bitter laugh escapes the girl. The police. One of the men who fucked her last week, brutally, was a policeman. Whatever is happening, the police will not help them. She knows.

9
BEAST

"Rock didn't tell us he wasn't comin'."

Dragon, the president of the Outlaw Sons, is not happy Rock isn't here.

"Rock sent me instead." Angel's voice is firm. There's no room for questions in it. "I represent him in his absence. I speak for the club."

We're standing outside a barn at a property just inside Lords of Carnage territory. About a dozen Sons are assembled behind their president. I wouldn't be surprised if there are others around that we can't see. A van with the logo for a plumbing company sits off in the distance, its suspension hanging low to the ground.

"You gonna tell me why your prez couldn't be bothered to tell me he wasn't comin' himself?" Dragon snarls. The single braid of his beard twitches as he speaks. It's a stupid affectation, that fuckin' braid. It makes me want to yank it off his face. Right before I punch him.

Angel hesitates for a split second. Any sign of weakness on the part of an MC prez is always a risk with a rival club. On the other hand, Rock's not showing up with no explanation is a sign of disrespect.

"Medical issue," Angel finally says. "Nothin' serious, but unavoidable."

Dragon smirks. "That right? Well, I suppose the old guy is gettin' up there in years."

The contempt in his voice makes my muscles tense. On either side of me, I can feel Thorn and Gunner's postures grow rigid.

"We're here to discuss terms," Angel says coldly. "So, let's discuss terms."

Off to the side, one of the Outlaw Sons —a meaty guy with a shaved head and a wide scar running across the front of his skull — lets out a bark of laughter. My right fingers start to curl into a fist, but I stop them.

"Rock tells me it's time for your club to get back into the gun business," Dragon begins pleasantly. The asshole grin on his face tells me he thinks he's got the upper hand in this conversation. "We'll see."

"Depends on the terms." Angel shrugs slightly, his eyes flicking to the van. "You're the one with the product. Let's see if you can make it worth our while to help you move it."

Dragon's eyes grow angry. "Rock and me already came to an agreement."

"Well." Angel doesn't move. "Let's make sure that *agreement* hasn't changed."

Angel doesn't trust Dragon. I don't fuckin' blame him. I was pretty goddamn surprised when Rock first came to the club with this proposal, and I know I'm not the only one. We haven't done business with the Outlaw Sons in the past because frankly, they're a bunch of fucking assholes. And they have a history of being allied with our enemies. Even though our clubs have never gone head to head, we're not exactly what you'd consider friendly.

Rock brought the proposal to us at church a couple weeks ago. Told us Dragon had approached him with an offer designed to be too sweet for us to refuse. The idea was to be part of a pipeline transporting weapons between Cleveland and Pittsburgh.

The Sons want to work with our club because our territory lies directly in between their turf and the next link of the pipeline to the south. Without us, they either have to go east into Death Devils territory, or west. Either of which loses them time and money.

We're pretty sure the Sons used to run guns through these parts with the Iron Spiders. But when the Lords of Carnage and the Spiders got in a bloody war that resulted in us wiping the Spiders off the map, our club took the opportunity to expand into the southern part of the state. We even started a second chapter of the Lords of Carnage to the southeast of us. Now the Lords control all the territory from here south, to the state line.

Which means that if the Sons want to run through here, they have no choice but to come to us.

Rock was convinced a business partnership with the Outlaw Sons was a good deal for us, too. Not everyone's on board. But the fact is, we need the money. We know the routes. It's a win-win for the Lords.

Except that means we have to play nice with a club we hate.

"So." Angel crosses his arms in front of him. "Rock says you want to make it worth our while."

"Worth it for *both* of us." Dragon pulls out a smoke and lights it. "If you think your fuckin' club can handle it."

Angry rumbles resonate through our men. Angel doesn't take the bait. Tension in his shoulders is the only sign he's preparing for possible violence.

"You move our product. You take your cut," Dragon continues. "Rock told me this was all settled."

"Just outta curiosity. Who these guns goin' to?"

"We got shipments comin' in from the docks in Cleveland. Goin' to a couple organizations out of Pittsburgh. Brown, mostly."

"MS-13?" Angel asks.

"And Kings."

Behind Angel, Ghost snorts. "You're supplyin' to both sides of their war?"

Dragon leers, showing a set of stained teeth with some gold. "Spics wanna kill each other, what the hell do I care? Whatever makes us the money, brother."

"I ain't your brother," Ghost fires back.

"You got a problem?" The asshole to Dragon's left, with the Enforcer patch on his chest, takes a step forward.

I've had enough of this shit. I step forward too and move into a defensive position, my hand ready to go for my piece. "You gonna *make* a problem, fucker?" I snarl.

Brick, our own Enforcer, moves into position next to me. One of the Sons makes a sudden move to reach behind him. One of our men yells out a warning, and all at once, guns are drawn on both sides.

Adrenaline pounds in my ears. For a few seconds, it looks like this is gonna end very badly.

"Dragon!" Angel shouts in sharp voice. "Tell your men to stand the fuck down!"

"Get your men in line, *VP*," Dragon roars back. "Or we'll blow them off the goddamn map."

"This ain't the time or the place to start a fuckin' war, Dragon," Angel warns. "Let's talk about this one on one. *Tell your men to stand down.*"

His voice echoes in the silence. A bead of sweat trickles down my temple. My eyes dart from Outlaw to Outlaw, searching for the slightest movement, the slightest reason to fire.

Dragon clenches his teeth and gives Angel a look of suspicion, but slowly lowers his gun. He glances back and gives a brief nod, and his men do the same.

"Stand down, Lords," Angel says. We do as we're told, reluctantly. "Dragon. Let's talk." He lifts his chin over to the far side of the barn. Without waiting to see if Dragon will follow, he walks away from the group. As he goes, he cuts a sharp look at Ghost, our Sergeant at Arms. "You keep shit in line."

"Understood." Ghost doesn't look happy about it. I don't fuckin' blame him.

Dragon waits a couple beats, then slowly follows Angel to a point about thirty feet away. Their murmurs reach my ears, sharp and strained. I can make out a few words here and there. Next to me, Thorn listens, too, his jaw tight. I hear them talk percentages. Angel argues a point or two. Gradually, the tone shifts, becomes less angry and more businesslike. I let myself relax just a hair. But then I hear Dragon say something that doesn't make sense.

"And the other product?" he asks.

"What product?" Angel frowns, his eyes narrowing.

Dragon pulls back, and cocks his head at Angel for a few seconds, saying nothing. Finally, he lifts his chin and smirks. "Guess I must be thinkin' of another conversation. Forget I said anything."

A few seconds later, Angel and Dragon exchange an edgy handshake. As they walk back to us, Dragon barks out to a bunch of his men to drive the van inside the barn and unload the guns into the trailer we keep there. Angel comes back to us, and tells us the run down to the border will take place in a couple days, once Dragon has confirmed with his contact that we'll be making the drop.

"Somethin' about this shit stinks," I mutter, glancing over his shoulder at the Outlaw Sons as they work.

"It'll work," Angel reassures me. "We're good."

I hesitate, then decide to ask the question that's on my mind. "Rock tell you anything about another product we'd be movin'? I heard Dragon say somethin' like that while you were over there with him."

"No."

"Any idea what it is?"

Angel shakes his head. "I'll talk to Rock about it. Goin' over to the hospital after we get back to town."

"I'll be over there later. Maybe we'll cross paths."

Angel nods. He glances over at the barn, where the Outlaw Sons have finished loading the shipment from their van to our truck. "We done here?" He calls over to Dragon.

"Yeah." Dragon hawks deep in his throat and spits on the ground. "I'll expect an update when you've made the drop."

"You'll get one." Angel looks around. "All right, Lords. Lock this shit up tight, and let's get a move on." He flashes me a grin. "See? We're good. Easy peasy."

I don't say anything. I'm not worried about the gun transport. We can do that with our eyes closed. But there's something fucked up about this situation. I can feel it.

I just don't have any goddamn idea what it is.

10
BROOKE

After a dinner of cold turkey sub sandwich and a shitty night's sleep on a too-soft mattress, I'm sitting in the sterile breakfast area of my hotel. Sipping bad coffee, I chew on a stale bagel with cream cheese and try to tune out the news station blaring from the TV mounted on the wall.

I'm sitting at one of six tables. The only other non-empty one is occupied by an older couple that look to be in their late sixties or early seventies. The man is trying to read a newspaper while the woman talks to him. From what I can tell, they're visiting their son and daughter-in-law from out of town. The woman is angry that they put them up at this hotel rather than having them stay at their home.

"I mean, it's not like they don't have the *room*," she's huffing. "My God, we come all this way to visit our grandchildren, and we end up spending the whole trip sitting in our hotel room twiddling our thumbs." The woman waits for a response from her husband. When he doesn't give one, she continues. "She's never liked us, you know. Robbie wouldn't be behind this. It was her idea. I'm sure of it."

"Rose, it's fine," the man says tiredly. "We saw the kiddos all day yesterday. Besides, I'm not going to complain about not having to sleep on a little kid's bed that's two feet off the ground and six inches too short."

"That's beside the point." The woman waves her hand at him as though waving away his words. "The point is, they don't *want* us here. *She* doesn't want us here. After all we've *done* for them. We practically paid for their *wedding*!"

The couple continues their bickering, and I stop listening and turn my attention to the day ahead of me. My first stop should be the laundromat again, to check whether they're open. Last night I spent some time searching for information about who owns E-Z Wash Express. I found the business in the state's database, with the owner listed as an M. L. Stephanos. No first name, just initials. Plugging his name (assuming it's a him) into a search engine yielded no results. Whoever this person is, he or she has no online presence. He's not in any FBI database, either. It's possible this is a squeaky-clean luddite who stays far away from computers. It's also possible the name isn't real.

Before I try to visit the laundromat again, I need to see if Chief Crup's babysitters are out there waiting for me this morning. And I could use some exercise to work out the kinks from that lousy night's sleep. I decide to kill two birds with one stone and go for a run. Dumping the last of my coffee and bagel, I go upstairs to my room and grab my running clothes out of my bag. I put on a pair of shorts, my sports bra and a T-shirt, and my running shoes. Pulling a headband over my head to keep my hair out of my face, I slip my key card into a small concealed pocket in my shorts and head out the door with my ear buds and my phone.

The highway that my hotel is on isn't exactly conducive to a pleasant run, but I seem to remember that if I take it about half a mile into town, there's a side road I can turn onto that will lead me into a quiet neighborhood. I do a few stretches leaning against a wooden bench outside the front door of the hotel, then start off at a slow jog to warm up my muscles.

No police car pulls out of the shadows to follow me. It looks like the Tanner Springs PD has decided to leave me alone this morning. Maybe following me to a sub shop yesterday proved boring enough that they lost interest. I increase my pace a couple of minutes into my run, and spot the side street I want to turn down. The street ends up being busier than I thought it would be. It's wider than I remember — practically a highway in its own right. Maybe there's some development on the other end of it that has increased the traffic. Thankfully, there's a fairly generous shoulder, so I move over onto the dirt and gravel and keep running. I'm on the left-hand side of the road, and cars pass by me, close enough for me to feel the wind as they pass, but not close enough to worry me.

I see the street that leads into the neighborhood and turn in. I start to pass by a series of tidy, medium-sized homes, with large leafy trees in front of them. As I run along, I remember that a childhood friend from elementary school used to live down here. Amelia, her name was. I picture her long straight hair and her red glasses, and recall how she used to have an American Girl doll collection I envied. I remember coming over to her house to play a couple of times. Until her mom found out who my parents were and where we lived, and decided Amelia couldn't play with me anymore.

A heavy feeling starts in the pit of my stomach. Amazing how something like that will still upset you, all these years later.

I take a deep, cleansing breath and blow it out, then turn up the volume on my music. I increase my pace, as though by running faster I can run away from the ghosts of my past. I finish my run through the neighborhood, purposely avoiding the street that Amelia's old house is on. By the time I get back onto the highway, I'm breathing heavily and streaming with sweat.

Glad to be on the home stretch as my feet pound along the dirt and gravel, I start daydreaming about how good a shower will feel. I'm praying that the room I'm in will have good water pressure when my right foot comes down half-on and half-off the raised blacktop. With a yelp of surprise, I go down hard. Falling sideways, my hip lands on a large piece of gravel, right on the bone. The pain is so sharp that for a second it immobilizes me. Tears spring to my eyes and I let out an involuntary cry, doubling over.

Dimly, I realize part of my body is actually lying in the road. I force myself to slide myself completely onto the shoulder while I wait for the pain from my hip to recede. When it does, I realize I've hurt my ankle, too, though I can't tell how badly. I inhale and exhale slowly, breathing through the pain, and try to flex my foot. A flare of fire shoots up my leg, making me grit my teeth and wince. I can move it, at least, so it's not broken. It might be sprained, but if I'm lucky it's just twisted. I decide to sit here for a few minutes before I try to walk.

Just then, a motorcycle comes over the hill off in the distance. The distinctive thump of its engine tells me it's a Harley. I look up, and notice the rider isn't wearing a helmet. His long hair flies out behind him as he rides. I can't help but think he looks a bit like Travis.

Then as the bike gets closer, I realize why.

It's because it *is* Travis.

Shit.

Crazily, I find myself glancing around for someplace to hide. As though I could just roll into the drainage ditch and he wouldn't see me. But it's already too late. It's clear he's recognized me. And even worse:

He's slowing down.

"Dammit," I mutter under my breath. "Dammit, dammit, dammit."

Travis stops the bike about five feet from where I'm sitting. He cuts the engine.

"This ain't no road to be runnin' on," he growls, frowning in disapproval as he looks me over.

"Uh, good morning to you, too," I shoot back. "And funny, I seem to have a memory problem. I don't remember asking you to come here and give me your opinion."

Travis swings a leg over his seat and climbs off the bike. He walks forward a couple of steps, until he's towering over me like a giant. "What the hell are you doin' sittin' there? Waitin' for a bus?"

I roll my eyes. "If you must know, I twisted my ankle. I'm just resting it for a few minutes before I try to stand up."

"You're gonna get mowed down by a truck, sitting there."

"I'm sorry I didn't choose a more convenient place to twist my ankle," I snap. "I guess I should have consulted you first." He's glaring at me like I'm some sort of stupid kid. It makes my blood boil, even though he's right. This isn't the safest place to be sitting. But that doesn't make me any less irritated with him.

"You should have at least had the common sense not to go running on a highway."

I snort. "That's pretty funny, coming from someone who doesn't bother to wear a helmet."

I expect that to piss him off, and get ready for him to yell at me. But to my surprise, one corner of his mouth goes up in a grudging smirk. "Maybe. But that's my choice. Not yours."

"So only men get choices?" I counter. "You get to choose to risk splattering your brains all over the pavement every time you ride, but I have to ask permission to choose a running route?"

Travis shakes his head and sighs. "I see the years haven't made you any less of a pain in the ass." He reaches a large hand toward me. "Come on. Let's see if you can stand up."

I consider refusing, but in the end I decide this momentary détente is better than outright hostility. I reach up to accept his offer. His strong fingers wrap around my hand, enclosing it in a grip I know could crush every bone if he had a mind to. At the contact with his skin a rush of memory bursts into my brain. Suddenly I'm seventeen again, and he's taking my hand for the first time.

Stop it.

Frowning with concentration, I plant my good foot firmly. And then, with a surprising gentleness, he raises me up, as though I'm no lighter than a feather to him.

Once I'm standing, balancing on one foot, he doesn't let go. Instead, as I face him, he takes hold of my opposite shoulder with his other hand, to steady me.

"Try to put your foot down," he says.

His deep baritone is so achingly familiar. It calls up memories of a time when I thought that maybe — just maybe — there was someone in the world who could love me just the way I was. Someone I could trust with the most broken parts of me.

A little shudder of longing passes through me like an echo, but I push it away.

Gingerly, I place my right foot on the ground. Travis's grip tightens on my shoulder as I try to put weight on it. A needle of pain goes up my leg and I wince, but it's not as bad as I feared. I freeze for a second, then put a little more weight on.

"I don't think it's sprained," I tell him, relieved. "Just wrenched it a bit."

"Good deal," he nods. He doesn't take his hand off my shoulder. Now that I'm not so worried about my ankle, I'm starting to be very aware of how sweaty and gross I probably look right now.

"Well," I continue, a little awkwardly. "Thanks for stopping. I mean, you didn't have to." I look up into his eyes, for the first time, really. Those electric blues stare back at me, unreadable. I feel my sweaty cheeks flush and resist the impulse to look away.

"You shouldn't be walking on that," he murmurs. "Not until you can put it up and get some ice on it."

"It's okay. It's not far." Actually, the prospect of walking the final three quarters of a mile back to the hotel is daunting, but I can make it if I go slowly enough.

"Fuck that. Come on."

The hand that's still holding mine tugs softly as he takes a step toward his Harley. Instinctively, I pull away, resisting.

"You need me to carry you?" he asks.

"What? No!" I squawk.

"Well then, come on."

"I don't need you to give me a ride, Travis."

"I'm not letting you walk back." His jaw goes hard.

"I'm a grown woman," I fire back. "You don't *let* me do anything."

"Do I have to pick you up and put you on the bike myself?" he threatens.

"You wouldn't dare," I snap, but even as I say it, I *know* I'm wrong.

"You wanna try me?"

I huff in irritation. "The years haven't made you any less pig-headed, have they?"

That gets a laugh out of him. "More, if anything," he growls, giving me just the hint of a grin. "So knock it off and come on."

He looks at me expectantly. When I don't move right away, he leans over and bends down as if to pick me up.

I let out shriek. "Okay, okay!" I protest, feeling ridiculous. He gives me his hand again and I lean into it for support. I take a hobbling step forward. Then another. Then another. Finally, when I'm standing next to the bike, Travis lets go of me and straddles the seat.

"Put your hand on my shoulder for balance," he instructs, and watches as I clumsily lift my injured leg over the back. He waits until I've managed to situate myself and put both feet on the pegs.

"Where we goin'?" he asks.

"Oh! The Courtyard Hotel." I wave a hand in that direction.

Travis fires up the bike. As he puts it in gear, it lurches forward a little, and I instinctively grab onto his waist for support. My hands slip under the leather of his motorcycle vest, settling on the soft cotton of his T-shirt. I can feel the hard muscles of his stomach and the heat of his skin through the fabric.

Something stirs inside me: a primal, physical reaction that weakens my knees and causes my breath to speed up before I even realize what's happening.

I lean forward against Travis, feeling the muscles in his back work as he steers the bike. The whole way back to the hotel, I fight the fluttering of my heart and the heat pooling between my legs. I try not to think about how dizzying it is to be so close to him — even as I fantasize about sliding my hands under his shirt and running my hands along the skin of his muscled abdomen.

11
BEAST

I drive Brooke back to her hotel, tryin' and failin' to ignore the way her arms are locked around my waist. How she's snuggled up to me, her tits pressing against my back. Brooke always had this effect on me, even when we were teenagers. By the time we get there, I'm hard as a bat.

I pull the bike into the circular drive in front of the hotel doors, then cut the engine. She awkwardly climbs off of the seat, favoring her right ankle.

"Thanks," she murmurs grudgingly. "I guess I'm lucky you happened along."

She takes one step toward the door, limping. Goddamnit, I can't let her go in like that. "Hold up," I grumble. I pull the bike forward a few feet and put down the kickstand. "I'll help you inside."

"It's fine, Travis. I can manage."

"Nope. I'm comin' with you."

Brooke lets out an exasperated sigh. "And I suppose I don't have any say in the matter?"

She's pissing me off, but still, I can't help but laugh. "Well, considering I'm almost three times your size and you have a fucked up leg, I'd say the answer to that question is, *no*."

"Jesus Christ," she mutters, and starts hobbling toward the door. I get in front of her and hold it open to let her pass through. Once we're inside, she briefly stumbles on the edge of a rug, and I catch her arm before she falls. Brooke looks up at me and gives me a reluctant purse of her lips. "Thanks," she mumbles.

I let her lead the way to the elevator, where she punches the button for the fourth floor. Once we're at her room, she fumbles for her key card and inserts it in the little slot. The door's a little heavy for someone who can't plant both feet, so I push that open too, and let her go in before me.

Brooke turns around about a foot inside the room, and literally bashes her face into my chest.

"Whoa," I chuckle, grabbing her by both shoulders.

"I…" Her face flames red. "I don't remember inviting you in," she sputters, to cover up her embarrassment.

"You're welcome," I shoot back. "Sit down on the bed and give me your key card. I'm gonna go grab some ice."

It's pretty damn obvious she doesn't want to, but to her credit she shuts up and does as I say. I take her card and grab the ice bucket sitting on top of the mini-fridge. It's got a plastic bag draped over the top of it, which I put inside the bucket and use to make an ice pack for Brooke's leg.

When I get back, she's propped up on her bed with some pillows behind her. Her left leg's on the floor, her right sticking out straight in front of her. I walk over and lay the bag of ice over her ankle as gently as I can. Brooke hisses as the coldness hits her skin, but doesn't complain.

"You sure it's not sprained?" I ask.

"No," she shakes her head. "At least, not badly. I just need to be off it for a few hours."

"Now will you admit you shouldn't have been running on that stretch of road?"

She casts her eyes up to the ceiling. "I could have rolled my ankle anywhere. It just happened to be there."

For a few seconds, neither one of us says anything. I tell myself I should take off.

"So," I ask instead. "What *are* you here for, Brooke? Some sort of FBI shit?"

She looks at me for a second, hesitating. Finally, she gives me a brief nod. "Yeah."

"What sort of shit?"

"A tip that was sent into our field office." She pauses. "Human trafficking."

"Seriously?" I ask skeptically. "Like, a sex ring?"

It's not like it's impossible. But it sure seems unlikely that something like that would happen out here.

"Yes, seriously."

"You get the shit end of the stick at your job, B, investigatin' something like that out here?"

My nickname for her slips out before I realize it. If she notices, she doesn't say anything.

"Yeah, maybe." She laughs softly. "My boss isn't exactly my biggest fan."

"You found anything yet?"

She smirks at me, one eyebrow shooting up in amusement. Something in her face reminds me of old times. It makes my chest hurt.

"I'm an FBI agent, Travis," she chuckles. "I'm not at liberty to tell a civilian the details of the case I'm investigating."

I snort. "Civilian. That's what we call 'em, too."

She frowns. "What?"

"People who aren't in an MC," I explain. "We call them civilians."

"Ah," she smiles. "Well. I guess we're both members of an exclusive club."

"That's one way to put it."

For a second, neither one of us says anything. The silence turns awkward, and Brooke looks down at the bedspread and clears her throat.

"Travis," she murmurs, her voice soft. "Thank you again, for helping me. And…" She stops, swallowing once. "I'm sorry. About… you know. The past. Everything." Her voice is tinged with regret. Brooke takes a deep breath, and then blows it out. "I had my reasons, for leaving the way I did. I know it was a shitty thing to do."

My jaw tenses. It's fuckin' surreal standing here right now, hearing her say this. Never thought I'd see this girl again, that's for sure. Much less get an apology from her.

I've been holding on to a lot of anger at Brooke Brentano over the years. Even as I told myself at the time I didn't give a shit. But the fact is, she's the first girl I ever felt anything for. The *only* one, to be honest. Hell, at the time I even thought I was probably in love with her. And I guess I fooled myself into thinking she might be in love with me, too.

But I was young, and filled with the kind of foolish bullshit that young people believe. For Christ's sake, we never even got past third base. I spent my senior year with a perpetual case of blue balls. At the time I told myself it was all worth it, because eventually Brooke would say yes, and then we'd be together.

And hearts and flowers, and unicorns and rainbows, or some such shit.

Jesus.

When she left, and I finally started to get over her — after shoving my dick inside so many women I literally lost count — I told myself she'd done me one hell of a favor, leaving town and ghosting me before I got in too deep.

And I believed it, too. I believed the hell out of it.

Just like I believed I'd never see Brooke Brentano again in this lifetime.

Now, here she is, right the hell in front of me. And the fuck of it is, hatin' her was a lot easier when she was an abstract idea.

"Yeah, well." I say gruffly. I don't want to see where this conversation is about to go. "We all have our reasons for doin' what we do, I guess."

Brooke stares up at me, looking like she wants to say more. It almost seems like she's sorry to see me leave, but I know that must be my imagination.

"Okay, then. I'm off," I tell her. "I gotta go visit someone in the hospital." I was on my way to see Rock when I ran across Brooke. It's not like I had a pressing appointment or anything, but it's an excuse to get me the hell outta here.

"Thanks again, Travis." Her eyes meet mine, and for a moment it's like we're locked together. Something passes between us — a current of what used to be. My dick jumps in my pants, and in spite of myself I have to fight the urge to close the distance separating us. To take her into my arms, and see whether the electricity that used to arc between us is still there. The pull is almost magnetic. But I don't move. I make myself stay put.

Brooke's mouth is half open, her breathing shallow. As I turn to go, her eyes fall to the patches on my right pec.

"Beast," she reads. Her voice is soft, curious. "Why do they call you that?"

I say the first thing that comes to my head.

"It's a reminder," I tell her. "And a warning."

12
BROOKE

Travis's parting words ring in my ears as I sit in bed icing my foot.

"It's a reminder. And a warning."

Beast.

Somehow, the warning suddenly seems like the universe is directing it at me.

As much as I wish I could lie to myself — as much as I wish I could pretend otherwise — my unexpected encounter with Travis just now has gotten under my skin much more than I wanted it to.

Yesterday, seeing him after all these years was unpleasant. More than unpleasant: it was excruciating. The anger and hostility radiating off him when he realized it was me was terrible. I wanted to sink into the ground and disappear. It took a supreme effort just to put on a shell of indifference and wait for him to leave the diner.

But as awful as yesterday was? Today was almost *worse.*

At least yesterday, I *knew* Travis hated me. I knew he'd do anything he could to avoid me while I was in town. And as bad as it was to have to see him again, at least it ripped the Band-Aid off and got it over with. There was almost a comfort in having the whole ugly episode in my rearview mirror.

Now?

Well, now, I have absolutely no idea how he feels about me anymore. Beyond probably thinking that I'm an incredible klutz who's too dumb to figure out a safe place to run. I mean, he definitely seems to still have some anger toward me. But if he totally hated me, he never would have stopped to help me in the first place.

Or insisted on driving me back here. Or helping me upstairs. He even got me ice for my ankle.

Why would he do that?

Don't be ridiculous, Brooke. He was just being nice.

Yeah, maybe. But a guy who has more tattoos than God and is a member of what looks to be an outlaw motorcycle club isn't likely to do things just to be *nice.*

Groaning, I fling myself onto my side on the mattress in frustration. I actually wish I could go back to being sure he hated me. Because that way, my traitorous brain wouldn't start thinking ridiculous, impossible things.

Things like imagining what would have happened between us if I'd never left Tanner Springs.

Things like imagining what might have happened just now if Travis had never left my hotel room.

I remember the first time I ever saw him. I was twelve years old, and he was riding around on a dirt bike on the gravel roads of our mobile home park. I'd never seen him around before, and I'd lived there all my life, so I was pretty sure he wasn't from the neighborhood. I watched him silently from the safety of my front yard, in awe of this boy who seemed to embody everything that was effortlessly cool to a girl my age. He was handsome, and athletic, and just seemed imbued with a confidence I was sure I would never possess. He never once looked in my direction that day as he rode around and around. I probably would have died of embarrassment if he had. He seemed like the kind of kid who led a charmed life. Like he didn't have a care in the world.

How I envied him.

My home life wasn't exactly ideal, which is probably why I was given to fantasizing about how other kids lived. It wasn't so much that we were poor, although I took my share of being made fun of by the richer kids for the second-hand clothes I wore. I could deal with that, though. What made my home a rough place to be that summer was that my mom had recently taken up with a man who drank. And when he drank, he sometimes hit her. Stephen — who my mom encouraged me to call my stepdad — would often stay out until all hours of the night with his buddies at the bar. When he came home, sometimes he was angry and spoiling for a fight. On those nights, the noise of him yelling at my mom would wake me up — and sometimes the neighbors, too.

A lot of the time, though, when he came home he was quiet. And when he was quiet, every once in a while, he would come into my room. At first, he'd just come in and stand by the door, and I'd pretend to be asleep. But eventually, he'd start coming further in. One night, he sat down on my bed, my thin mattress sinking under his weight. He reached under the covers. His rough hand brushed against my leg. When he touched me, I froze. Paralyzed, I lay there in terror as he slid his hand forward and touched me in a place no one had ever touched me before. I was still pretending to be asleep, but he whispered to me that I could never tell my mom about it. That she'd never believe me anyway.

That night, after he finally left my room, I lay awake, scrunched up in a little ball, and wished I was a boy. A boy who could fight, and defend myself. A boy like the one with the dirt bike, strong and confident.

But then, I'd realize that if I was a boy, I might grow up to be a man like my stepfather. A man who would touch little girls in their sleep.

I told myself that not all men could be like that. It wasn't possible. Some of them had to be the kind who would never do what Stephan had just done.

But the problem was, I didn't know if it was true.

I didn't see Travis again until almost four years later, when I was a sophomore in high school and he was a junior. I noticed him one day outside the front doors to the school, before first bell. He looked so familiar, but it took me a few seconds to realize why. He'd grown, of course — he'd gone from a still-gangly thirteen year-old to a tall, handsome seventeen. He towered over the other kids in his grade, and seemed older than even the seniors. His voice had deepened, too. I remember being struck, again, by how at ease he seemed. How his peers deferred to him, out of respect and maybe a little fear. I found myself staring, just as I had the first time in the mobile home park. Only this time, somehow Travis must have felt my gaze. Because suddenly he turned in my direction and locked eyes with me.

And *winked.*

Oh, God, I was humiliated. I was convinced he was winking at me like an adult winks at a child. He seemed years and years older than I was, and so… *manly.* By comparison I felt small, and impossibly young. I fled inside the school building seconds later, feeling silly and ridiculous. I avoided him like the plague after that.

That's not to say I didn't think about him. I definitely did. Travis was the first boy I ever fantasized about. I would construct elaborate daydreams about him being secretly in love with me. I imagined him kissing me — closing my eyes and pretending by touching my lips to the skin of my forearm. He was the boy whose heart I wanted to capture, more than anything.

And, miracle of miracles, I did.

But by that time, it was too late.

By that time, I had discovered the hard way that underneath every man's harmless exterior, there lies a beast.

And now, the universe is back, with a reminder that Travis is no exception.

* * *

An hour later, my foot is feeling better. Which is a relief, because I am already sick to death of flipping through cable channels trying to keep my mind off Travis.

Tossing the remote onto the bed, I stand up and test putting weight on my right ankle. There's a little twinge, but nothing major. I take a few experimental steps. I'm still limping a bit, but I think it will probably be fine by morning.

My stomach is rumbling, so food is going to be an issue soon. I decide to break my normal rule about fast food and go through a drive-through. And after that, I'll head over to the mini-mall and see whether the laundromat is open today.

Since I'm still covered in dry sweat after my run, I take a shower, wash my hair, and do a quick blow-dry with the hair dryer the hotel has provided. I almost get dressed in the suit I was wearing yesterday, but at the last second I decide that if the laundromat is open, I want to do a little recon before I pay them an official visit. So instead, I throw on a pair of jeans and a T-shirt from my bag. Then, because I don't have any dirty laundry to wash except the running clothes I was wearing earlier, I pull the comforter off the bed and strip the sheets.

Tossing my running clothes into the middle of the pile, I wind the sheets into a ball and tie the ends together to make it easy to carry. I go to the safe in the closet and pull out my pistol and holster, strapping them on. Finally, I root around in my bag for a zip-up hoodie and throw that on to cover up the gun.

I take the stairs down to the first floor. It's slow going since I'm still limping, but I don't want one of the hotel staff to see me and think I'm trying to steal their linens. I go out one of the lesser-used side entrances of the hotel and toss my bundle in the back of my car. When I get to the mini-mall, instead of stopping right away, I do a first pass by the laundromat. I see that it looks open today. I make a right at the next street and turn around, then enter the parking lot from the other direction. Parking my car a few doors down, I get my laundry from the trunk and go inside.

The place *looks* like a functioning laundromat, at least. There are rows of washers in the middle of the room, and some high capacity machines along the wall to one side. On the other side is a bank of dryers. The appliances look to be on the older side. I wonder if this place has been here since I was a kid. I have no memory of it, but that's not too surprising. The mobile home park I lived in was over on the far north edge of town. I wouldn't have come here to do laundry even if it was open back then.

I'm unsurprised to see that there aren't any other customers here doing laundry, given the lack of cars in the lot. At first, I think I'm the only person in the place, but then the sound of something slamming in the back tells me I'm not alone. Realizing I need to start acting like a customer, I look around for a change machine, and am just feeding a five-dollar bill through the slot when a withered-looking woman with frizzy goldish-red hair and drawn-on eyebrows comes out of a door in the back. I don't make eye contact, just get my change and go over to one of the washers. After a moment, she seems to lose interest in me and goes back out through the same door.

Now that I've been seen, I decide it's probably best to actually do this load of laundry. I check the controls and select the shortest cycle. I put my sheets and running clothes in, then settle in to wait.

I spend the next half-hour fiddling with my phone and drinking a warmish diet Coke I bought from the machine next to the change dispenser. When I get bored with that, I flip through some ancient magazines I find on a folding table. No customers come in. The only person who enters from the front is a heavy-browed man in his early twenties, who scowls at me as he passes and goes straight through to the back.

My wash cycle ends, and I pull everything out and start the dryer cycle. The heavy-browed man comes out of the back and leaves, not looking at me at all this time. I walk around the place, scanning for anything unusual or unexpected. I notice the business license taped to the wall by the front desk. The owner is listed as M.L. Stephanos.

I wait until the dryer cycle is almost finished. There's been no sound or movement from the back room in quite a while. Quietly, casually, I wander toward the back, past the closed door the woman went in. Beyond that, there's a long hallway. The place is bigger than I thought from the outside. It seems to take up the entire L-shaped wing of this side of the building. There are other doors in the hallway, all closed, made of heavy wood. I try a few; all are locked.

I arrive at the end of the hallway, and see there's a stairway leading down to a basement. Taking a quick look backwards, I silently descend the stairs.

It's dark, but I don't dare turn on a light switch. Instead, I get out my phone and find the flashlight app. When I turn it on, I see that the basement is massive, and empty. Strangely empty, in fact. There's basically nothing in here at all. No old machines, no shelves for parts, no laundry orders. It seems weird that they'd have all this space available and not have anything in it.

I walk around the perimeter, stepping quietly and sweeping my phone flashlight around. As I do, I start to realize that the space, as well as being empty, seems oddly clean. There's not really any dirt on the floor, or cobwebs, or anything like that. In a way, it looks less unused, and more… recently vacated. Maybe it's my overactive imagination, but it just doesn't feel right to me.

Then, as I'm passing the light across the floor, a small silver circle flashes in the darkness. I walk over and bend to look at an object stuck in the corner.

It's a ring. A cheap one, costume jewelry. The bauble on the top is iridescent, a small round bubble with shimmery flakes inside it. It looks almost like a tiny snow globe, frozen in time.

As I reach down to pick it up, footsteps sound on the stairs. I grab the ring and shove it into the back pocket of my jeans.

Lights come on, illuminating the entire basement in a dull, yellow glare. "What the hell are you doing down here?" the old woman snaps.

"I'm so sorry," I stammer, thinking fast. "I was looking for the bathroom."

"Are you stupid?" she spits. "Bathroom is upstairs. First door on the right."

"I'm sorry," I repeat. Quickly, I walk to the stairs and start climbing. "I guess I must have missed it somehow." I flash her a bright smile. "Weak bladder."

I hurry past her before she can ask me any more questions. Once I'm back upstairs, I rush down the hallway and find the bathroom. I close myself in and lock the door, then make myself pee. After I flush, I make sure to make plenty of noise washing up and using the hand dryer. I go back out into the main room of the laundromat, where the woman is now standing at the front desk, glaring at me. I go to my dryer and open it. I still have five more minutes left in the cycle, but the sheets are dry enough. Grabbing them into a ball, I head for the front door, nodding a hasty goodbye to the woman.

I drive straight back to the hotel, going back in through the side entrance. Once I'm upstairs and in my room, I toss the laundry in a heap on the bed and take the ring out of my pocket.

Sitting down in the lone chair next to the window, I hold it up and stare at it, twirling it around in my fingers and watching the sun hit it as I think.

It's dark inside the back of the truck. There are no windows, and the single door that rolls down is closed and locked. The girls sit on the floor. They slide around as it moves, grasping at one another for purchase.

The ride is bumpy. The truck turns, first this way, then that. They had left the basement hastily, and the two men who herded them into the truck in the first place seemed rushed and angry. The girl has no idea where they are going. None of them does. A few are scared, and cry. But for most of them, wherever they are going now can be no worse than everything that has already happened.

After a few minutes, the truck slows, then stops. They don't seem to have gone far. They hear slams, and then the back door rolls up. The girls who have been crying and wailing stop. Their breathing hitches as they work to be quiet, to not call attention to themselves.

The men tell them to stay where they are, and to shut up. Outside, there are no lights, and only the noise of crickets. They've driven out of the town. As the girls sit in silence, the men stand a few feet away from the truck, smoking and arguing. The girls can only make out a few words here and there, but it sounds like they cannot agree on where to take the them.

They stay like this in the truck for many hours. Some of the girls fall asleep, Katya among them. Eventually, one of the girls who has stayed awake finds the courage to call to the men, asking to go to the bathroom. A couple of the others raise their hands as well.

The girl does likewise — partly for the chance to stand up and stretch, but also because she has learned that things like bathroom breaks do not always come when needed.

The men allow six girls to climb down off the truck, in pairs, and go off into the bushes to pee. When it is her turn, her partner timidly asks the men if there is any toilet paper. "I have to go number two," she murmurs in broken English. The men yell at her and tell her to use leaves.

The girl goes into the bushes, moving far enough away from her partner that she hopes no one will hear her peeing. She does her business, but instead of standing up, she pulls up her underwear and moves a few feet away to sit down on the ground. It is the first time she has been outside and alone in months. She runs her hands through the grass and dirt. She trembles, realizing that the last time she did this was before. *In another country, on another continent.*

When she was free. Before she knew anyone's life could be as bad as hers is now.

The men have started arguing again. Silently, almost without thinking, the girl lifts herself into a crouch and begins to run. As she does, she prays that the other girl who went into the bushes with her takes a long time to do her business. For as long as the other girl takes, the men will not think to look for her. They will not know that she is gone.

She runs, as silently as she can. Her fear threatens to choke her, but she keeps going. As she does, she thinks of her friend Katya, still asleep in the truck.

I'm sorry, Katya, the girl repeats in her mind. Tears fall from her eyes, stream down her face, but she does not wipe them away as she stumbles blindly through the brush.

I'm so, so sorry.

13
BEAST

The next day, I'm just turning into the hospital hallway where Rock's room is, when I see something that stops me in my tracks.

Coming out of Rock's room is the mayor of Tanner Springs, Jarred fuckin' Holloway.

It's such a surreal image that for a second I can hardly believe my eyes. Holloway *hates* the Lords of Carnage. Or rather, he loves to blame the Lords for what he's fond of calling the "unprecedented crime wave" that supposedly hit Tanner Springs about a year before he was elected. It's what he campaigned on, creating all manner of boogeymen to make the citizens of our fair city freak the fuck out and start locking their doors against us at night. Even though Tanner Springs was, and still is, one of the safest towns around — mainly because of our club. The Lords have done our bit to keep order in the city limits, because the less crime there is here, the less heat and attention there is on us.

Which leaves us freer to do what we please, *outside* of town and in the confines of our clubhouse.

So, Holloway gets elected on this "holy hell, it's a crime wave!" fake bullshit — which he *knows* is fake — and then after his election, he gets to sit back and announce that crime has gone down and the streets are safe again. Meanwhile, he and the police force he packed with his toadies do absolutely fuck-all, because they don't *have* to.

I gotta hand it to Holloway, he's a lazy piece of shit, but a clever one.

Holloway doesn't see me right away, since as soon as he's out in the hallway he pulls out his cell phone and starts tapping on it. By the time he looks up, we're almost eye to eye. He startles for a second, but then almost instantaneously, his mask slips into place. His mouth contorts into a polished smile of even white teeth. I've seen him give that exact same smile to pretty much every person in Tanner Springs. I wonder how many of them notice that his smile never reaches his emotionless, dead-fish eyes.

I have a sudden impulse to punch him, just for the pleasure of it, but somehow I resist. It ain't worth the headache, even though I know it'd feel goddamn fantastic. I don't bother making casual small talk with him, because Holloway knows I can't fuckin' stand him. Instead, I narrow my eyes and sneer at him, altering my path so I come just a little closer to him as I pass. His shitty politician's smile falters and he darts to the side. When he's safely past me, he clears his throat and keeps walking like nothing happened.

Jesus Christ, I hate that little prick.

Rock's alone when I get to his room.

"What the fuck was Holloway doin' in here?" I ask as I come in, jerking my thumb back toward the hallway.

"What?" Rock looks up sharply, seeming alarmed, but then after a second he lets out an abrupt chuckle. "Oh, yeah, that. He just had the wrong room. Came in here by mistake."

"You sure about that?" I cock my head at him. "I don't trust that fucker as far as I can throw him. Though I could probably throw that asshole pretty damn far. Preferably through a plate glass window." I grab a chair and flip it around, then sit down and rest my elbows on it. "You want the club to station someone outside, to stand guard? Keep old Holloway from making any more 'mistakes'?"

"Nah," he waves me off. "It's fine. I'll be gettin' out of here soon, anyway. The doc says if I take it easy I can probably leave tomorrow."

"That's good news." I reach up to my pocket for a smoke, but then remember where I am. "You had any visitors today?"

"Thorn's here," Rock replies. "He's down at the cafeteria, gettin' some coffee with Isabel on her break."

I grin. "He visitin' you, or her?"

Rock snorts. "Good damn question."

"How you feelin'?"

"Like shit. But don't tell them that, for Chrissake, or they'll never let me leave." He shifts in the bed, wincing a little. "What's the word on the drop for the Outlaw Sons? Everything good?"

"Yeah. It's been pushed back a little, though. We're goin' out there in a couple days. Angel's on top of things. Don't worry, Rock, it's handled."

But Rock doesn't seem reassured. "We'll see," he grunts, his brow furrowing.

I figure he's feelin' pissed being cooped up here and having to let Angel do his job, so I don't say anything more. Instead, I distract the prez with news about what's been goin' on at the clubhouse. I tell him how much shit Lug Nut's been gettin' lately for showin' us the yoga moves Eden taught him. "Everyone's been callin' him Yogi ever since," I say, and Rock starts laughing so hard I feel like maybe I'm not supposed to get him so worked up. "He might be lookin' at a change of road name, whether he likes it or not."

Rock's still chuckling quietly when the door swings open behind me. Isabel comes into the room dressed in her nurse's scrubs, followed by Thorn.

"Hey, brother. Isabel." I stand. "What's up?"

"The coffee in the cafeteria is a goddamn abomination, that's what's up." Thorn's face is contorted with disgust. "Sweet baby Jesus, I don't know how they can get away with sellin' that shite. There should be a law against offering something so vile to people whose loved ones are sick."

Isabel laughs softly. "You do get used to it. Which, to be honest, is probably not a good thing."

I look at her and motion to the seat I just vacated, but Isabel shakes her head. "I can't stay," she says, glancing up at Thorn. "He's claimed all my break time. I should be getting back."

"I'll walk you out, then," I reply. "I'll let Thorn have a turn with the old man."

"Fuck you with that old man shit," Rock says irritably.

Thorn shoots me a grin. "You headin' to the clubhouse?" he asks me.

"Eventually. But I thought I'd drop by Twisted Pipes first."

"All right. I'll see you."

Thorn pulls Isabel to him, giving her a long, deep kiss that goes on just long enough for Rock to clear his throat. "Okay, okay. That's enough of that bullshit," he mutters, only half joking.

Thorn snorts and releases Isabel, who rolls her eyes playfully at Rock. "You," she points at him. "Get some rest. And you," she continues, turning to her man, "Don't overstay your welcome. Rock might look fine, but he's still in here for a reason."

I go out into the hallway with Isabel. As we walk down the hall, I notice she looks tired, and her face is pinched. Even though her job is hard, she's usually smiling and happy when she's here at the hospital. But not today.

"You okay, Iz?" I ask her. "You don't seem yourself."

"I'm fine," she says, her voice strained. "I'm just a little upset. I was telling Thorn about this in the cafeteria. A girl was brought in a little while ago. She's young, maybe fourteen or so. Doesn't really speak English other than a couple of words. She was barefoot, no identification. Barely even dressed." Isabel's face is covered in worry. "I think she might have been locked up somewhere. Like a slave," she says. "And from the look of the clothes she came in wearing, I'm afraid I know what kind of slave."

"Shit. Are you for real?" My mind instantly goes to Brooke, and why she's in town. "Sex trafficking?"

"It seems like it," she nods sadly. "She sure wasn't wearing a maid's uniform."

"Holy shit." The gears in my head start to turn. I run a hand through my hair, thinking. "Isabel. Could you take me to her room?"

"I'm not sure that's a good idea, Beast." She looks suddenly uncomfortable. "I probably shouldn't have talked about this with you. Or Thorn, for that matter. It was unprofessional of me."

"Come on, darlin'." I put my hand on her shoulder and look down into her sad eyes. "Look, I got a reason for asking. I know someone who's in town right now. Someone who's here investigating a trafficking tip. A fed."

"Are you serious?"

"Yeah. I am."

I watch her as she processes what I've just told her. "Wow," she murmurs, lost in thought. "I was thinking that once we managed to find someone who speaks her language, we should probably call the police. But we're not there yet. We're still trying to track down the blue phone."

"What blue phone?" I ask, puzzled.

"The CyraCom." She looks up at me. "It's a blue bag, with this blue phone in it, and a booklet. The booklet has a message in it, written in a bunch of different languages. When you have someone who doesn't speak English, and you don't have an interpreter for them on hand, you have the patient look through the book until they recognize their language and point at it for you. Then we can call a number on the blue phone, and we'll get an interpreter in that language to help us communicate with the patient."

"Huh," I say, impressed. "That's a pretty fuckin' cool idea."

"It is," she nods. "Especially for smaller facilities like ours, who don't have a lot of people on hand who speak different languages. Hospitals are required to have one. But we hardly ever use ours, so no one knows where it is. It'll turn up, I'm sure. But in the meantime, we just have to wait, and treat her as best we can." Isabel bites her lip. "I just hope she knows how to read."

"Look," I say, making a decision. "I'm gonna go talk to this person I know. If it's what you think it is, this girl deserves to have someone listen to her story. And you and I both know that the Tanner Springs police are worthless." I look her in the eye. "We good on this?"

Isabel takes a reluctant breath. "I'm not the person to make that decision, Beast. But as of now, she's just a patient with no identification being treated for minor cuts and bruises and exposure. We're not barring people from visiting her. So…" she shrugs. "I mean, your friend can come try to talk to her, and unless the girl refuses, the hospital won't stop him."

"Her," I correct.

She raises an eyebrow but doesn't comment. "Okay. I better get back to work. Oh, and Beast? Don't ask for her room number at the information desk. They won't give it to you." Silently, she mouths: *Three-oh-four.*

"Got it. I'll be in touch."

14
BROOKE

The morning after my visit to the laundromat, I contemplate my next move as I work out in the hotel gym.

I'm forcing myself to take a break from running until I'm sure my ankle is totally healed. Instead, I make use of the machines and free weights set up in one corner of the room. A lone guest walks on a treadmill in front of a TV playing morning shows while I listen to my favorite workout playlist and do renegade row pushups and deadlifts.

I mull over going back to the laundromat and asking to speak to M.L. Stephanos. But after yesterday, I know the woman working there will recognize me right away. There's no way she won't figure out I was snooping around in the basement. She's not likely to tell me a damn thing.

I've checked the Better Business Bureau and done a property tax record search online with the county. The name of record for the property taxes is an LLC with a post office box in New Jersey. At this point, I'm coming up with a lot more questions than answers. My next plan is to go to the county in person and flash my badge, but I'm not sure what that will turn up. It seems whoever is behind M.L. Stephanos and his laundromat is working hard to keep the secret.

In frustration, I turn up the volume on my earbuds and blast my way through three more sets of arm exercises. By the time I'm finished, I'm sweating profusely and no less frustrated, but at least I've burned off some energy. I wipe off the equipment I've been using, grab a fresh towel from the stack by the door, and take the stairs back up to the fourth floor as I mop myself off. I'm still breathing heavily as I heave open the fire door and step into the hallway.

And notice a large, leather-clad figure leaning against the wall opposite my room.

I hate more than anything the way my heart starts to race at the mere sight of him there. And oh God, I hate that once again, he's seeing me bathed in sweat, my hair sticking to my beet-red face. If this is karma for something I've done in a past life, whatever it was must have been *bad.*

"You know," I say, to cover up my embarrassment, "It's not a good idea to stalk a federal agent."

I expect Travis to toss back some smart-ass comment. But instead, he stands up and turns to me, his face drawn and serious. "I've got something for you," he says, not even realizing he could make a sex joke out of a remark like that. "Something big."

When Travis tells me why he's come, though, all thought of jokes and laughing — even sex — flee my mind. I ask him to wait downstairs for me while I take a quick shower. I change into my suit, leave my gun in the safe, and twenty minutes later, I'm striding into the hotel lobby. Travis is sprawled out on one of the generic, uncomfortable-looking couches in the middle of the room. I catch the woman behind the front desk eyeing us suspiciously, and almost laugh. It'd be hard to find two people who look more mismatched at the moment than we do.

"I'll follow you in my car," I say as Travis stands.

"Fuck that," he growls. "Come on. We'll take my bike. I'll drop you back here afterwards."

It's not a request. I should protest, but he's already out the door before I can say anything. His bike is out front, in the spot where he parked it when he brought me back after I twisted my ankle. He fires up the motor and glances back at me impatiently to get on. Realizing resistance is futile, I climb on behind him, feeling a secret thrill as I wrap my arms around his waist.

"Sorry I don't have a helmet for you," he calls above the engine. "Didn't have time."

When we get to the hospital, we stop just outside the front doors. Travis pulls out his phone and punches out a text. A second later, he gets a response. "Isabel's gonna meet us at the elevators on three."

We go up to the third floor. When the elevator doors open, a strikingly beautiful, olive-complected woman is there to greet us. Her long dark hair is pulled back in a high pony, and she's wearing nursing scrubs.

"Hey," the woman says, taking a step towards us. She looks at Travis and nods, then turns to me. "I'm Isabel," she murmurs, holding out her hand.

"Brooke."

"I'm sorry," she hesitates. "Would you mind showing me your badge?"

"Of course." I pull it out and flip it open, holding it up so she can examine it. When she seems satisfied, I put it away. We start to walk down the hallway, Isabel slightly ahead of us.

"We've located the blue phone," she begins. At my frown, she explains. "It's a way to connect patients with interpreters remotely. I showed the girl the booklet, and it turns out, she speaks Ukrainian." Her wide eyes are full of concern. "I believe her name is Natalia. We're going to try to contact an interpreter who can ask her to tell us what her full name is, whether she has any family she wants us to contact, and what happened to her that she ended up here." She takes a breath. "Once we've done that, I'll ask the interpreter to tell the girl who you are, and whether she'd be willing to answer your questions."

"That sounds perfect," I agree.

"Beast." Isabel turns to him. "I'm thinking, maybe it would be better if you stayed out of the room for this? If she's… well, if any of our suspicions about her are right, it might be easier for her to talk to us if there were just women there."

"Got it." He nods once. "I'll go down to the cafeteria and have some of that shitty coffee Thorn loves so much."

Isabel gives him a grim smile. The two of us watch him as he heads back to the elevators.

"Thank you for doing this," I say.

"I'm doing it for the girl," she replies. "Please don't make me regret it. And if she refuses to talk to you, that's the end of it. FBI agent or no, if she doesn't want to tell you anything, you'll have to get some sort of warrant or something and go through the official hospital channels to come back. I won't have that on my conscience."

"I understand." And I do. I admire this woman for taking such a strong stand.

We continue down the hallway in silence. "How do you know Travis?" I ask.

"Travis?" She wrinkles her nose in confusion.

"Um… Beast, I mean."

The corners of Isabel's mouth quirk up. "His real name is Travis?" she asks.

"Yeah. I knew him back in the day. High school."

"Wow. That's…" She laughs, shaking her head. "It's hard to picture him as a high school kid."

I have to smile. "He looked similar. Not quite as tall or as big, though. Or as many tattoos."

"I'm with one of the other Lords. Thorn."

"Aha. Hence, how you know him as Beast."

"Yeah, that's how pretty much everyone knows him now. I've never heard him called Travis before."

We arrive at the girl's room, and Isabel knocks softly on the half-open door before peeking in. "Hello, Natalia," she says slowly and deliberately.

"H-h-ello," the girl repeats softly.

She looks so tiny, there on the bed. She's in a flimsy hospital gown that is giant on her, and she has the covers pulled up around her waist on all sides, like she's trying to make a fortress. Remnants of makeup stain her eyes and cheeks, but beneath it she could be anywhere from twelve to eighteen. More on the younger side, I think, and my heart aches at the idea. Her eyes are like saucers, huge in her thin face. There is a light bruise on her left cheekbone, and some cuts on her arms. She's pale, and clearly afraid, but otherwise she doesn't look seriously hurt.

Isabel steps forward and picks up a blue bag that's sitting on a chair. She unzips it, and takes out a strange-looking phone with two headsets on either side and a bank of buttons in the center. Pulling a cord out of a side pouch, she connects one end to the phone and another to a jack on the wall behind the girl's bed.

Isabel picks up a laminated sheet that's resting on the small stand next to the girl's bed. "I'm going to call someone who speaks your language," she says slowly, pointing first at the sheet, and then at the phone. The frowns for a second, then seems to understand, and nods. Then her eyes flicker toward me, as though noticing me for the first time.

"This is…" Isabel begins, and then hesitates for just a moment. "…A friend," she finally finishes. I flash her a grateful look.

"Natalia?" I ask. The girl stares at me, and then does the same brief hint of a nod. "I am Brooke," I say, pointing my thumb at my chest. "Natalia." Pointing at her. "Brooke." Pointing at me.

"Brooke," she repeats quietly. I give her what I hope is a reassuring smile.

"That's right." I look over at Isabel.

"Okay, here goes," she says. She sets the phone on the small table with wheels next to the bed, and pushes it close to Natalia. Picking up the left handset, she pushes a blue button on the phone itself, then listens. A few seconds later, she pushes a white button beside it.

"Ukrainian," she says into the mouthpiece, slowly and distinctly.

She waits. The room is quiet. Then:

"Hello, interpreter. I'm a nurse at Tanner Springs General Hospital. I have a patient here that I need to get some general information from. She came to us without identification, and she does not have any friends or family with her… Yes. Yes. Here she is."

Isabel picks up the other handset and gives it to Natalia, who puts it to her ear.

"*Sluchaju?*" she whispers.

And then, as Isabel and I watch, she bursts into tears.

The interpreter gives the girl a minute to collect herself. Natalia clings to the phone like a lifetime, sobbing, "*Diakuju! Diakuju!*" over and over into the phone. I'm struggling not to start crying myself, to imagine how terrified and alone she must feel, and what a relief it must be to talk to someone who can understand her.

Little by little, Natalia quiets. The interpreter must say something to Isabel, because she wipes at her eyes and clears her throat. “Yes. Yes. Natalia. Please tell me what your full name is, and where you’re from.”

Isabel listens, pulling a pad and pen from her pocket to write notes. Through the interpreter, she finds out that the girl is from a town outside Kiev, and that she is sixteen years old. She was taken from the streets of Kiev months ago.

“Natalia. What brings you here to the hospital? Where did you come from?”

In a halting voice, the girl explains that she was locked up in a place with other girls. That they were being used for sex by the men who came there. She says that they were in that place for a long time, but that yesterday, or maybe the day before, they were woken up in the middle of the night and told everyone was leaving. They were put into a truck and driven away. Natalia managed to escape when she asked to go to the bathroom and ran into the night before they realized she was gone.

Natalia’s voice has been rising as she speaks, her tone growing desperate.

“Ya ne znav kudy yty! Ya boyavsya! U mene nemaye dokumentiv! U mene nemaye hroshey!”

The girl begins to weep, her head buried in her hands.

“Isabel,” I say quietly. “Can you please ask the interpreter to tell Natalia who I am, and ask her if she’s willing to talk to me directly? Please tell her that I want to help the girl. I want to make sure she's safe."

Isabel talks into the receiver. The girl listens as the interpreter speaks to her. Then, sniffling, she looks over at me and nods, wiping her nose with the back of her hand.

"*Tak.*"

Isabel hands the phone to me. I spend the next ten minutes or so getting as much of Natalia's story as I can. I ask the names of her parents, and how to get hold of them. She tells me her mother is dead, but that her father is alive and lives in her town near Kiev. At the end, I tell her that I will make sure she's safe and that I'll help her get back home. She starts to cry again and thanks me, over and over.

Isabel takes the phone from me. "Tell Natalia to rest, now," she says to the interpreter. "We're going to keep her here overnight, and I'm going to contact the Ukrainian embassy and have them get in touch with her father."

Natalia listens to the interpreter, clutching the handset tightly. Tears spring to her eyes once again, but for the first time, they're not from fear. She looks at me and gives me a smile so hopeful, so innocent, that my heart feels like it's going to shatter.

The call ends. I glance over at Isabel, who looks as wrung out as I feel. As she starts to replace the blue phone in the bag, a soft tap on the door makes all of us turn our heads.

Travis steps into the room. “Hey,” he rumbles. “Everything good in here?”

From the bed, Natalia begins to scream.

15
BEAST

The girl's yelling her head off when Brooke hustles me out of the room and closes the door behind me.

"What the fuck is wrong with her?" I mutter, bewildered. "She was lookin' at me like I murdered her whole family."

"I don't know," Brooke whispers urgently. "Maybe it's just that you're a man and she's afraid of men in general right now. But I'm going to see if we can get the interpreter back on the phone and ask Natalia what's wrong."

I wait out in the hall, resisting the urge to go outside for a smoke. About twenty minutes later, the door opens again. Brooke steps outside. Her face is drawn and pale.

"So, what's up?" I ask. "Did you figure out what was freaking her out so much?"

"Yeah."

"Well? What is it?"

Brooke bites her lip. For a second, she refuses to look at me. When she finally does, it's with eyes full of suspicion.

"It's your cut," she bites out. "Natalia says one of the men who came to rape her sometimes had one just like it."

"You mean one *sort* of like it," I correct her.

"No. She said the same one." Brooke is looking at me with something like hatred. "She said she recognized some of the same words."

"What the fuck? That's not possible!" I explode, my voice rising to a shout. "The Lords do *not* deal in that kind of shit, Brooke. Absofuckinglutely *not*."

"You can't tell me your club is a bunch of choir boys, Travis," she cries. "How do you expect me to believe you — *any* of you — would stop at this?"

"No, we're not choir boys! I wouldn't pretend otherwise!" It makes my gut twist that she thinks I or any of my brothers would be capable of raping a girl who can't be more than sixteen. I have to know she believes I'm a better man than that. "I know you're not naive, Brooke," I say, working to keep the anger out of my voice. "Yes, the Lords get up to some shit that's not strictly legal." I shrug. "Sometimes people get hurt. But the people who do get hurt are other MCs, other clubs who cross us. Not civilians." I grab her by the shoulders, my eyes boring into her. She doesn't resist. "And not little girls, Brooke. *Jesus*, not little girls."

Brooke looks at me for a long time, here eyes not leaving mine. "How do you explain what Natalia says she saw, then?" She finally asks, in a tired voice. "She's not lying, Travis."

"I know." I shake my head. "And I don't know what the explanation is. But somethin' ain't right."

Brooke lets me lead her out of the hospital. She's quiet, and pretty obviously upset. I don't know if I've managed to convince her one of the Lords would never do what that girl said. I have to admit, the situation's pretty damning.

But I can't imagine any of my brothers would fuck a girl who looks so young, who can't even fuckin' speak English. I go through them one by one in my mind. Not even Sarge, the sickest motherfucker of us all.

"Natalia will need some clothes," Brooke murmurs as we exit outside into the sunshine. She seems like she's talking to herself more than anything. "And a place to stay once the hospital releases her."

"We can head over to the clubhouse," I suggest immediately. "Ask one of the women if they'd have some stuff that fits her."

"The look on her face, Travis," Brooke whispers then. It's like she didn't hear me. Her breath hitches in her throat as she stops to stare at me. "She was absolutely terrified. That poor girl is…" A stifled sob stops her words. She covers her hand with her mouth, shaking her head violently as she tries not to cry.

"Babe." My arm is around her shoulders pulling her close before I realize it. Suddenly, it's almost like all the years between us have just slipped away. For a second, her body tenses, and then she seems to melt into me. "It's rough, I know," I murmur. "But she's safe now. She's okay."

"Travis." Brooke buries her face in my shoulder. "Please, please tell me this has nothing to do with your club."

"It doesn't," I insist.

It *can't.*

I put Brooke on the back of my bike.

And then, against my better judgment, I drive a fuckin' FBI agent to our clubhouse.

There aren't a lot of brothers around when we get there. Bullet and Lug Nut are playing pool in the back. Striker and Tank are hunched over a deck of cards and a bottle with two shot glasses at a table in the corner. They give me a nod as I come in, their eyes darting in curiosity to the chick in the suit who follows behind me.

"Jewel," I call out as I lead Brooke to the bar. "Grab me a couple of beers and come over here."

"Sure thing." Jewel goes and gets a couple of bottles, then flips the tops and comes over to set them in front of us.

"This here's Brooke," I say.

"Nice to meet you." Discreet as ever, Jewel doesn't give any indication that Brooke's appearance is at all strange. "You look like you could use this," she says, pointing at the beer.

"Yeah, I suppose I can," Brooke sighs, and picks it up. She takes a long drink, tipping her head back to expose her throat. I try not to get hard at the thought of how much I suddenly want to kiss her there.

"So what's up, Beast?" Jewel says. "You wanted to talk to me?"

"Yeah. Got a favor to ask."

I start to tell Jewel about the situation, trying to leave out the details so I won't be steppin' on Brooke's professional toes. But to my surprise, Brooke takes over the story and starts to explain who the girl is, that she's in the hospital right now, and that she needs clothes because she escaped from a sex trafficking operation that Brooke is trying to track down. At first, I'm surprised as fuck that Brooke's giving this kind of info to a stranger. But then I realize she might be tryin' to see whether Jewel will give away any reaction that would show she sees a connection to the club.

Jewel listens and nods, raising her eyebrows sympathetically. "Oh, my God. That poor kid," she murmurs. "You said she's from Ukraine?"

"Yes," Brooke answers. "And unfortunately, she doesn't speak very much English. We had a phone interpreter through the hospital to get her story, but I'm afraid she probably feels pretty isolated now, with no one to talk to."

"My neighbor is from Ukraine," Jewel muses. "Olga. She's a really sweet lady, when she's not on my ass for playing my music too loud." She looks at Brooke. "Do you think this girl would like to have a visit from her?"

Brooke blinks. "Wow," she says, considering. "She would probably love it. I'm going to be contacting the Ukrainian embassy to get hold of her dad, but even so, it will take some time to deal with all the paperwork and things to get her back home. I'm sure she'd be thrilled to see a friendly face who speaks her language."

"How big is she?" Jewel asks. "I can run home and grab some clothes, then go talk to Olga before the men start coming in to party later."

"She's about my height, but skinny," Brooke explains.

"I'll bring her some stuff to wear that's cheerful, without being revealing." Jewel's eyes shine with sympathy. "So she can feel comfy and safe."

I tell Jewel to get in touch with Isabel about bringing the clothes to Natalia at the hospital. She steps out from behind the bar and announces to the room that she's leaving for an hour or so. A minute later, we hear her car firing up from the parking lot outside.

"She's nice," Brooke remarks as the engine recedes into the distance.

"She'd give a stranger the shirt off her back," I reply, and then chuckle. "Which I guess is pretty much what she's doing."

"Travis," she continues, shifting on her bar stool. "You know that with what Natalia said about recognizing your cut, I should be looking into that." She looks around the room.

"Brooke, I stand by what I said," I rumble. "Our club is not involved in that shit." Part of me is pissed at her for even thinkin' it, but I can't say I blame her. I take a swig of my beer and think for a moment, frowning. "I'll talk to our vice-prez about it, though. See if he has any ideas what she saw."

"Your *vice*-president?"

"Yeah. Our prez is out sick right now. Heart attack. Our VP's in charge until he gets back on his feet."

While we've been talking, Brooke has completely drained her beer, even before I have. I suppress a chuckle. The girl's been wound tight as hell today. I guess she needed the release.

"Want another one?" I ask, nodding at her bottle.

She sighs. "I should call the embassy," she says, shaking her head.

"So, call them now." I shrug. "The beer will be waiting for you when you get done."

I expect her to protest, but she only hesitates for a second before standing. "Okay," she agrees. "I'm gonna go outside for a couple of minutes."

"Take your time. Anyone asks who you are, tell them you're with me." Brooke looks about as out of place as the Queen of England at a pool hall. It may be the first time anyone has ever worn a suit in this place.

While she's gone, I grab us two more beers and sit there, thinking about everything that's happened today. And how fucking surreal it is that Brooke Brentano is sitting here next to me having a beer like the last twelve years never happened. When she comes back in, she's removed her jacket, and seems just a little bit less out of place, if you don't look too close. She sits down and we talk some more about Natalia, but then pretty soon we're just talking about anything, whatever comes to mind. I ask her about how she likes working for the FBI. She shrugs and says it's fine but not like she thought it would be. When I press her for details, she refuses to answer and changes the subject. She asks me about what it's like to be in an MC. I tell her it's a hell of a lot different than working for the fuckin' FBI. She starts to laugh then, a full-throated, carefree sound that reminds me of old times. My throat gets a little tight at how good it sounds.

Brooke is looking looser and happy by the time her second beer is finished. With a grin, she lifts her butt off the seat to go grab us two more, but I stop her.

"Whoa, there. You drink much more and I won't be held responsible if you fall off the back of my bike."

"I'll take my chances," she shoots back.

"Nope." I stand, making a decision, and put my arm around her. "Come on. I'm gonna get you home."

Brooke is quiet as she pulls on her jacket and I lead her out of the bar. She doesn't protest, but she doesn't seem happy about it, either. She doesn't say anything as I get on the bike, just slides on behind me and wraps her arms around me. She's silent on the way to the hotel, too, but I can feel her breathing, shallow and rapid, as her chest rises and falls against my back. The nearness of her does to me what it always does, and I'm uncomfortably hard when we pull into the hotel.

Instead of dropping her off in front, I park in the lot and get off the bike with her. She's still pouting a little as I escort her inside, and she doesn't break her silence until we're getting out of the elevator on her floor.

"You know, I didn't need your help to find the room number," she snarks as we walk up to my door. "I might not be as big as you, but I'm not *that* much of a lightweight."

"That's not why I came up," I say, watching her slide her key card through the slot.

"Why, then? My ankle's all better, didn't you notice? I'm not even limping anymore."

I push the door open to let her through, then follow her inside. "That's not why, either."

"Then what…"

By the time the door slams shut behind us, I have her pressed up against the wall. My cock is still hard as steel as I pull her against me.

"Because I've been trying like hell not to do this for three days, and I'm about at the end of my rope," I growl against her ear. "And if I'm not mistaken, you are, too. Am I wrong?"

Brooke shudders at the feel of my breath on her skin. She shakes her head. I feel her hair brush against my cheek as she does.

"No," she whispers. "You're not wrong."

I reach down, lifting her until her legs are wrapped around me. She moans loudly and arches her hips so that her softness presses against my hardness.

"Let go, Brooke," I rasp against her neck. "Let go of whatever it is you're trying so hard to control."

"Oh, God, Travis," she gasps. Her body takes over, and she begins to rock against me. Sweet Jesus, this has been twelve long years coming, but it's about to come, *hard.*

"Fuck," I groan as my mouth comes down on hers. She opens to me, eagerly, as I devour her. I pull her away from the wall and carry her to the bed, the two of us falling down onto the mattress together.

"You want this? You're sure?" I need to ask it, even though her body's already given me my answer.

"Yes," she pants. "Travis. I need this." She pulls back, her wide, dilated eyes locking on mine. "I want to forget everything. Please, make me forget for a while. I want to be dominated."

16
BROOKE

"You want this? You're sure?" he asks.

It sounds almost like a warning. I think back to what he said about his name.

And maybe it *is* a warning. A warning that once we do this, there's no going back to the way things were before. This is uncharted territory.

But I don't care.

"Yes," I hear myself say. "Travis. I need this. I want to forget everything. Please, make me forget for a while. I want to be dominated."

I didn't mean to say it — I didn't mean to say *any* of it. But it's true. I want to be erased, taken, *ravished.* I want him to make me forget my own name. For once, I just want to give myself up to pleasure, and not be afraid of losing control, or being afraid, or hurt. I want it to be like I didn't leave him all those years ago.

I want to make up for years of wondering what I gave up when I ran away from him.

Travis and I were never really together — not like that. We were headed that way, for sure. But after what happened — after what made me leave town — I was too afraid to let him touch me again. Even Travis, who seemed to actually care about me. He didn't seem like the other men I knew. Even though part of me believed that being with him would be amazing — perfect, even — a bigger part of me couldn't handle how crushing it would be if I was wrong.

If Travis turned out to be an animal.

It's almost too ironic. I ran from the man, and now I'm flinging myself back into the arms of the Beast, with no idea what I'm getting myself into.

But I'm about to find out.

"I'm gonna make you come, baby. I'm gonna make you scream," Travis rasps against my ear. The tightness in his voice tells me he's been waiting for it, too. His words make me moan again, the sound ripping from my throat.

"I just…" I gasp, and then words just start to come out of my mouth. "I just want this. So bad. I wanted this so bad, Travis. I'm sorry I…"

"Shhh." He hushes me with a rough kiss that leaves me breathless and panting. "It's not about the past. It's just about now."

It's exactly what I need to hear. My body takes over, just like it couldn't all those years ago. Travis leans into me on the bed, his hard length pressing against my aching center in *just* the right way. I moan into his mouth as I arch toward him, the delicious pressure and friction making my heart pound. I could come, just like this, I'm sure of it. My core is throbbing, soaking with heat and need.

Travis groans, and then chuckles. "You're so fuckin' wet, babe."

Instantly, I freeze, mortified. I must be soaking through the fabric of my pants. My face flames, and I start to push against him, but he anchors me in place. "That's not an insult, Brooke," he growls, staring at me with hooded eyes. "It's fucking hot. I can't wait to taste that sweet pussy of yours."

Oh, God. How can talk that filthy be so embarrassing and so *hot* at the same time? I feel myself grow even wetter, which I would have thought was impossible. Every nerve ending in my body is singing, practically pleading with Travis to touch me and relive the pressure that's building inside me like a fire hose.

He raises himself up to his knees and pulls off his cut, tossing it to a chair by the bed. Then as I watch in fascination, he peels off his T-shirt to reveal an intricate curling of tattoos that trace up and down his arms and onto his chest. Most of the designs are black ink, but there's one on the left side of his chest that makes me stop and gape at it in amazement.

It's a beast. A dragon, probably. The artwork is beautiful. But the most stunning thing about it is the orange fire that breathes from its mouth.

It's *gorgeous.*

In fascination, I reach up and touch the ink. Travis's skin is hot, the muscles under the tattoo hard. As I run my fingers down his chest, he draws in a sharp breath. I continue, slowly, down the path between his strong abs, toward the top of his jeans. Just beneath the zipper, his cock is pulsing.

I reach forward with my other hand and undo the button with trembling fingers. My mouth is actually watering with the need to taste him. I've done that before, to a few men, but I've never liked it. But with Travis, I want to. I lift myself up onto my elbow as I start to tug at his zipper.

"You're gonna have to leave that for another time, babe. Right now, I've got other things in mind."

In an instant, Travis is up off the bed, towering over me. "Take off that suit, Brooke. I want to see you naked and ready for me."

Feeling self-conscious, but also incredibly turned on, I do as he says. I kneel on the bed and take off my jacket, tossing it to the floor. My silk blouse goes next. Then I slip over to the edge of the bed. Kicking off my shoes, I unzip my pants and wriggle out of them, until I'm standing before him in just my bra and panties.

Travis gives me a long, lingering look and pushes his unbuttoned jeans down to the floor. His cock springs free, thick, hard, and huge. It's monstrous, the biggest I've ever seen. He takes hold of it and begins to stroke, openly admiring the view. He lifts his chin at me, his eyes not leaving my body. "Take off the rest."

He pumps himself, slowly, as I undo the clasp on my bra and push my panties to the ground. The air is cool against the wetness coating my sex and my upper thighs.

"Touch yourself," he commands.

I open my mouth to protest. I've never done this in front of anyone. For a second, it occurs to me that he's trying to humiliate me — that he'll laugh at me, find me ridiculous. But one look at his hungry eyes and my mouth snaps shut again. He wants this. He wants to make me do his bidding. And that's what I asked him for. I asked him to take control.

So I do as he says.

I reach down with a tentative hand and slide a finger against my slick folds. The touch makes me shiver in spite of myself, and my eyes half-close in pleasure. I want Travis to make me come, but this feels so good I can't help but stroke myself, softly, my hips involuntarily moving forward in rhythm to meet my hand.

"Fuck," Travis grunts. He starts to stroke faster. "Pinch your nipples. Do it," he orders when my eyes dart to his.

I take my right nipple between my thumb and forefinger and roll it. The jolt is intense, a lightning bolt sent straight to my clit. I gasp, loudly, and throw my head back.

"That's right, baby," he murmurs. "Just like that."

"Travis," I moan. "Please."

"This is just for me, babe. Your turn is coming soon."

I force my eyes open and lock my gaze with his. I realize the only way I can get him to give me relief is by pushing him further. Biting my lip, I continue to stroke myself, cocking my hips and rolling them toward him. It's a provocation.

It works.

With a hiss, Travis abruptly slows the rhythm of his stroking. Sliding my eyes down his body to his cock, I see a bead of precum leaking from his tip.

"That's good, baby. That's real good. Now lie down on that bed and spread your legs."

I'm almost drunk with relief, so much so that I hardly manage to be embarrassed that he wants me in such a vulnerable position. I climb on the bed and lie on my back, spreading my legs like he told me to. My breath is coming in shallow bursts of anticipation. Travis kneels on the mattress, sinking it down, and before I realize what's happening he's pushed my legs even further apart and his head is between my thighs.

"Oh, my…" I start to gasp, but my words end in a sharp cry as his mouth finds my clit.

His tongue is hot, insistent. He licks and devours me as I writhe on the bed, already so close I know he could finish me with two or three quick strokes. But he takes his time with me. He slides himself deep inside me, tasting, then draws his tongue out and uses my juices to tease and torment me. I know I'm crying out, begging him, but my mouth has a mind of its own just like my body does. He's in total control, and we both know it. The jolts of electricity running through me turn into flames. My body arches like I'm being tortured, but it's the sweetest torture I've ever known.

"Travis," I whisper then, just as a feeling like vertigo over takes me. "Oh, Travis, oh, God…"

The explosion rocks through me, stronger than anything I've ever felt, like an earthquake, like the end of the world. I'm crying out, and then he's inside me, pumping, filling me with heat, stretching me to the breaking point, possessing me, owning me. A blinding light of pleasure and pain consumes me as he pulls me forward, hands on my hips, then withdraws and thrusts deep inside me again, over and over. Then, I'm climbing again, and just as he shouts out my name I start to fall, into the abyss, into the forgetting. There's nothing but this, but him, but here. Now.

I fall into a dreamless sleep in Travis's arms. When I wake up, it's getting dark. The curtains are still open from the daytime. Fading light illuminates the room just enough for me to see that there's a note lying on the pillow next to me:

Didn't want to wake you.

No signature, no extra words. It's somehow reassuring how simple it is. No promises. No excuses.

I almost manage to convince myself I'm not disappointed.

I glance at the clock and see I should probably go and grab some dinner. Pushing away the nagging sense of sadness that I'm alone, I throw on some jeans and a tank top and set out in search of food. I'm not really in the mood to interact with strangers, so I decide to find something I can get as takeout.

I find a Mexican place and order some tacos to go. Then I drive around for a few minutes trying to find someplace to eat it so I don't have to go back to my hotel room. Eventually, I realize I'm close to Tanner Springs Senior High. I end up devouring the tacos in the parking lot of the upper campus, watching a few kids playing tennis under the street lamps on the aging court adjacent to the school. The kids look so young and innocent as they play. They're not bad — probably on the tennis team, I figure. These are some of the "good" kids — the ones who don't live in a mobile home park, and who have stable homes with a mom and a dad who encourage them to join teams and make the honor roll and pay for tutors to help them study for the ACT.

These are not the kids who would have been friends with a kid like me. Or like Travis, for that matter.

When I first saw him riding around our mobile home park on his dirt bike, I assumed he was a golden child who had everything he wanted, and not a care in the world. In reality, he came from a home not that much better than mine. The house he lived in wasn't much more than a shack, on the opposite end of town from our trailer.

He did have two parents who cared about him, though. And a big sister two years older. His dad worked in a factory the next town over, and his mom worked part-time as a cashier at a dollar store. I knew the family didn't have much, but Travis didn't seem to mind. He never complained about it, anyway.

I only found out about all this after Travis and I started spending time together, a couple of months into my junior and his senior year. One day after school, I was hanging around outside one of the side entrances of the school building — not far from where I'm sitting now in my car eating my tacos. I was supposed to go home right after school, but I was trying to avoid it.

Not the home at the trailer park. I didn't live there anymore.

In a foster home.

Over the summer, my mom had died. It was sudden and unexpected. A tear in one of her arteries from an undiagnosed heart condition.

Through the wall of my grief, it never occurred to me in those first few days what would become of me. My stepfather had left my mother almost a year before, so it had just been the two of us in the trailer. Somehow, I had just assumed that I'd be allowed to keep living there for a while. At seventeen years old, I figured I could take care of myself. I was even told by the lawyer that there was a small insurance policy that would come to me on my eighteenth birthday.

Unfortunately, until then, I was considered a ward of the state. A week after my mom's death, I was placed in temporary foster care with an older woman who seemed irritated to have me there. Then, right before school started, I moved in with Mr. and Mrs. Bonner.

And living with Mr. Bonner turned out to be even worse than living with my stepfather.

That day after school, I was sitting on a cement planter outside the building, wishing I had somewhere else to go than back to the Bonners'. The side door to the school opened, and out came Travis Carr. It was a thrill to see him, but terrifying at the same time. I sat frozen in place staring at my fingernails, too shy to look up.

"Hey. Brooke, right?"

I forced my eyes upward to meet his, hardly believing he knew my name. If anything, he'd gotten even more handsome over the summer. He could easily pass for twenty, and was more muscular and broad-shouldered than even most of the football players. Next to him, I still felt small and childish. I couldn't imagine why he was even bothering to say hello to me, when practically any girl in the whole school would have chopped off a limb to go out with him. I just assumed he was being nice to what he saw as a pathetic little kid.

"Yeah," I nodded reluctantly.

"I'm Travis."

I almost laughed. *Everyone* knew who Travis Carr was.

"You waiting for someone? You need a ride?" He jerked a thumb in the direction of the parking lot. "I can take you."

I can only imagine that I gaped at him in shock. It was beyond any fantasy I'd ever had about Travis — and I'd had a lot of them — that he would just offer to drive me home from school. But he acted like it was a totally normal thing to do. It was absolutely terrifying, and completely thrilling. It felt like I was dreaming.

Except I didn't want to go home. Not at all. But the prospect of being alone with Travis Carr, as nervous as the thought made me, was too good to pass up.

I mustered up all the courage I could find in my body, and stood up.

"Sure," I said nonchalantly.

What followed that day, and the days and weeks after that, was something I could never have imagined in a million years.

Travis Carr and I became *friends*.

He told me about his family. How his parents wanted him to go to college, but they couldn't afford it and he wasn't feeling it anyway. I told him about my mom's death, and that I was living with foster parents. I told him I hated it there, but I didn't tell him why.

He started picking me up for school a few times a week, when he didn't have weight lifting in the morning for the wrestling team. If he was ever embarrassed to be seen with me, he never showed it. I finally started to get less nervous and more comfortable around him, even though I still had a huge crush on him.

I told myself he was just treating me like a friend. Like a little sister, almost. In a way, that was comforting. Even though I wanted more — my *body* wanted more — I was afraid of my own desires. And worse than that, I was afraid of the desires of men.

Maybe Travis sensed that, somehow. Maybe he went slowly on purpose. And for a while, it worked.

But in the end, maybe he went too slowly. Or not slowly enough. I don't know. All I do know is, by the time we got close, I was too damaged to trust him, or any man.

In the end, I ran, because I couldn't face Travis anymore. I felt dirty, like I could never be clean. Like he would never be able to love me if he knew.

Today, I know better. At least in theory. I know I'm not dirty. But I am still damaged.

And I'm afraid that finally letting Travis in has opened a door to the past that I've been trying to keep locked for years.

17
BEAST

My hands still feel the warmth of Brooke's skin as I ride to the clubhouse. My tongue still tastes her.

I still hear her cries of pleasure in my ears. Still feel the release of my cock as I emptied myself deep inside her.

She let herself go with me. For the first time. She let go of her defenses and let me in.

And I know it was something she needed. I can still hear her, begging me to make her forget everything for a little while. Asking me to take control.

I always knew Brooke kept something essential about herself hidden from the world. Something she never told anyone. Not even me. When we were kids, she seemed strong as hell to most people. Independent, almost to the point of being aloof. But I knew underneath all that, there was something fragile about her. Something I needed to be careful not to break.

From the first time I saw her, Brooke was always gorgeous as fuck. She had this way about her, kind of a "fuck you" attitude wrapped in a sexy little body. But unlike other girls her age, she didn't feel the need to put it all out there on display. Hell, she might not even have known the effect she had on guys. Maybe she didn't see it, or maybe she chose not to see it. I don't know.

That day I ran into her outside the high school, sitting around by herself, she looked like a wild thing. Like a bird just about ready to take off at the slightest movement.

I was careful not to scare her off. Careful to give her time to trust me. To let her open up to me.

I thought I was getting there. I thought I was cracking that tough exterior.

And then she skipped town, without so much as a word or a look back.

I never knew why. Over the years, I thought about her from time to time. I always made myself stop, though. There was always a willing pussy I could forget myself inside. A willing mouth to give me what I needed, even if it wasn't exactly what I wanted.

Yeah, I was pissed at her for leaving. Pissed as hell.

Now I'm just pissed at myself. Because I know pretty soon she's gonna leave again.

And if I had just stayed the fuck away from her, I wouldn't care that much.

I left the hotel after she fell asleep, without saying goodbye. I know it's better that way. Because there's no way this shit has a future. Partly because Brooke was never the kind of girl to look behind her when she decides something's over.

And partly because in spite of what just happened between us, she's a fuckin' fed, and I'm in an outlaw MC. We live by different codes. Work under different creeds.

And right now, I'm on my way to deliver a shipment of illegal firearms. To be sold to rival gangs who won't be happy until they've managed to completely kill each other off.

* * *

The run down to the border takes a couple hours. Our contact is supposed to meet us at an abandoned gas station out in the middle of fuckin' nowhere. By the time we get there, we have a little over half an hour to get into positions, just in case shit goes bad. Bullet, Sarge, and Horse keep watch while Angel, Brick, and I pull the truck around the back of the station. The three of us get out and take a walk around the perimeter, then settle in to wait.

"Rock's outta the hospital today," Angel tells me as we lean against the truck. Brick is still walking around checking shit out.

"Yeah? Who's picking him up? He staying at the clubhouse again?"

"Nah." Angel lights a cigarette and blows out a plume of smoke. "I guess Trudy's givin' him another chance. She's pickin' him up at the hospital and takin' him back to their house. Maybe him almost dyin' made her re-think the divorce."

"Could be." Trudy and Rock's relationship is none of my fuckin' business, but I have to admit it would be sad if they can't make it work after all these years they've been together.

"Hey, Angel," I continue, changing the subject. "I got something to run by you."

"Yeah? What?" He gives me a glance.

"It's… kind of fucked up."

I got no idea how to start talkin' about this, so I might as well just come out with it.

"Okay," I begin. "The short of it is this. I was at the hospital yesterday, to see Rock. Happened to find out from Isabel about this girl that got brought in with injuries. Girl from Ukraine. Shows up alone, and it turns out she's only sixteen years old." I pause. "Well, come to find out, she escaped from this sex trafficking operation. She don't speak

English, so she barely knows anything at all. But she saw my cut," — I look down, and then nod at his — "and she freaked. Said she recognized it." I wait a beat. "Said a man with the exact same cut was one of the men involved with the trafficking ring."

"What?" Angel looks at me sharply. "That ain't possible. You sure she didn't just see a different MC's cut and figure it was one of ours?"

"That's what I said. But apparently, she insisted."

Angel frowns at me, skepticism etched in his features. "You said she doesn't speak any English. So how do you know that's what she said?"

Here's where shit gets complicated. But I have to tell Angel the whole deal. I explain about Brooke being in town. He doesn't remember her name — Angel's too old to have been in school with her. I tell him she's an FBI field agent now, and that she's in town looking into potential human trafficking in the area.

Angel's face freezes into a stony expression as I finish. "You've been talking to a fed," he says flatly.

"Yeah."

"This is the point where I ask you if you're fuckin' nuts, brother," he snarls.

"Look," I sigh. "Brooke used to be…" I stop for a moment, considering my words. "She used to be a friend of mine," I finally say. "She ain't here for the club, brother. She's here looking into some bad shit. She couldn't care less about what goes on with us."

"Except she has a fucking *witness* that literally just fuckin' *told* her that one of our men is part of this goddamn ring she's tracking!" Angel's voice rises in anger.

"But you know as well as I do that ain't the case," I retort. "It can't be. The girl had to be making a mistake. Look, it's lucky I was there to hear about this. This way, we don't find out about it when the feds raid our clubhouse looking for evidence."

Or maybe not. Maybe it's the worst fucking luck in the world that I was there. If the girl hadn't seen me in her hospital room, she would never have pointed the finger at our club in front of Brooke.

But the damage is done now. We gotta deal with it.

"Look. It's good that the club knows this." I repeat, looking Angel in the eye. "Maybe, I dunno… maybe I bring you to talk to Brooke. Or shit, maybe we investigate this on our own."

"Jesus fucking Christ," he mutters, tossing down his smoke. "I do *not* need this right now."

"Sorry, brother. I should have brought it up another time."

"No. No," he shakes his head tiredly. "Okay. Look. Let's talk more after this drop is done. I want to know everything. Every. Fucking. Thing."

Just then, Angel's phone buzzes. He pulls it out of his pocket and glances at it. "Bullet sees movement. They're coming."

Angel looks over at Brick and gives a short, shrill whistle. Brick nods back. Just then, an SUV pulls into the lot. I watch as the doors fly open, and four men jump out. Behind them, an old, beat-up pickup drives in. I glance at the truck to see how many men are in it, but something out of the corner of my eye flashes just as Brick yells something over to my right.

"Gun!"

I hit the ground just as a bullet sings by me, hitting the back of our van near the gas tank. I scramble behind a tire for cover and return fire. There's no time to think, no time to register any of my brothers' positions as a rain of fire power flies in both directions. I aim and shoot, then aim and shoot again, adrenaline rushing through my veins as I hit one of the men and watch him go down. Dirt and debris explode around us as the deafening sounds of our bullets echo in all directions. I hit another man, who hits the dirt and lies motionless, one leg twitching in front of him. It's a small victory, but the fact is, our handguns are no match for their semi-automatic rifles.

"It's an ambush!" Angel shouts.

I scramble to my feet and run behind the van. Off to one side, I see Angel's taken cover behind a cement pillar next to an old gas pump. He returns fire, giving as good as he gets. I can't see Brick, but I hear gunfire coming from the far side of the gas station so I'm assuming that's where he is. Bullets continue to assault us. One of the ambushers manages to shoot out a window of the van, and the glass shatters all around me, raining down like spiked hail.

"Motherfucker!" I shout, and pull myself up to look through the hole where the glass used to be. I fire off three rounds, quickly, then duck again. I don't know if I hit anything. But just as I'm pulling myself back down, I think I just glimpse something that makes blood run cold in my veins.

A familiar patch. One I'd know anywhere.

A skull, outlined with eight segmented legs, like the fingers on a skeleton. *Spiders.*

Moving fast, I dive into the passenger door of the van and reach for an AR-15 we keep mounted to a gun rack near the floor. I ram a loaded high-cap magazine into it and slide out, then lift myself up to the broken window again and start firing. I watch in satisfaction as one of theirs screams and falls back, half of his head blown off by one of the blasts. I keep shooting until the mag is spent.

Suddenly, the gunfire stops, leaving us surrounded by an eerie silence. In front of us, there's no more movement.

"Lords!" calls a voice from behind the trees. It's Bullet.

"Status!" Angel barks back.

"Men down! Enemy neutralized!"

Warily, I emerge from behind the van. Angel does the same. Guns still drawn, we step out toward the bodies on the ground in front of us.

"Brick!" I yell.

"Here!" he calls. A second later, he appears. "You all good?"

"Yeah," Angel shouts. "Got grazed, but I'm good."

Bullet comes out from across the road, limping. A dark blotch of red seeps through his jeans below the knee. His eyes are wide and angry.

"Sarge and Horse." His voice is husky, rough.

"What about them?"

Angel says the words sharply, as if daring Bullet to tell him bad news.

But Bullet just shakes his head.

"They're gone."

The three of us drive across the road and load Sarge and Horse's bodies into the van. Bullet's shot in the calf, so we leave him to watch over the bodies of the enemy. As I'm walking back across the road, I see Bullet aim and take fire into one of the dead men's chests.

"He still movin'?" I ask as I look down.

"Nah." Bullet hawks loudly, then spits on the corpse's face. "Just wanted to plug this motherfucker one more time."

"You all right?" I ask him, nodding toward his leg.

"I'll make it," he grunts. "Got some tampons to stop the bleeding. I always carry 'em since the first time I got shot."

I give him a grim laugh. "That's right. You still got that one lodged in you, don't you? Shit, you're gonna be settin' off metal detectors for the rest of your life."

"We'll see," he shrugs, his voice tight. "I'll let Smiley decide when we get back whether this one needs to come out."

Angel and Brick join us, the four of us staring down at the motherfuckers who killed our brothers.

"This means war," Angel says simply.

“Yeah,” Brick agrees. “And they ain’t left any doubt who the war is against.”

As we look down at the dead — at their patches — two things are clear.

The Outlaw Sons were never in this to do a deal with us. They were in it to *end* us.

Them, and what’s left of the Iron Spiders.

18
BROOKE

The next day I go to the hospital to see Natalia. Travis hasn't contacted me, and I don't expect him to. What happened yesterday was probably just a crazy, one-time thing. There's no reason to expect anything more.

I park my car in the hospital ramp and make my way down the corridors toward Natalia's room. I exit the elevators to the third floor and am turning down the last hallway, when a thirty-something man with slicked black hair and an expensive suit stands up from a chair in a waiting alcove.

"Special Agent Brentano," he intones. "This is an unexpected pleasure. May I have a word?"

He looks vaguely familiar, but I'm not sure why. He sort of has the appearance of a B-grade movie star. Like an actor on a TV show that's destined to fail after the first season.

"I'm sorry, have we met?" I ask politely.

"Not quite," he replies. Beneath the smooth tone, there's a slight edge to his voice — so slight I'm not sure if I'm imagining it. "I'm Jarred Holloway. I'm the mayor of Tanner Springs."

"I see." I look at his outstretched hand for a moment before taking it. His skin is dry and cool. Vaguely reptilian.

"Chief Crup told me that you were paying us a visit," he continues. He holds my palm in his just an instant too long. He squeezes once, tightly, before letting go.

"Yes," I say noncommittally. I've been in this town long enough that I'm starting to feel reticent about giving anyone any information about why I'm here. Especially this man. There's something… *off* about him. Something unpleasant. He's handsome, I guess, but in this weird, too-perfect way. His face looks like plastic. Like he's had work done. The result is vaguely robotic.

"He mentioned that you're working on an anonymous tip you received. Something about…" — he wrinkles his nose in a pantomime of disgust and disbelief — "*sex* trafficking?"

I'm beginning to seriously regret my courtesy call to Chief Crup.

But then I remember something.

I never told Crup what *I was investigating.*

The thought hits me like a thunderbolt, and I have trouble concealing the reaction. I force my face into a mask of neutrality and change the subject.

"Mayor Holloway," I ask. "Were you here at the hospital looking for me?"

"Oh, no, no." He raises a hand and smiles. One canine tooth in his smile is ever-so-slightly off. "I'm just here visiting a dear friend. Just a happy coincidence that I should run into you."

"Even more of a coincidence that you should know what I look like," I remark drily.

"This is a small town. Faces are familiar. A *newcomer*" — he raises one eyebrow at me playfully — "stands out fairly quickly."

"I see."

"How are things going? With your 'investigation'?" He says the word as though it's in air quotes. "If you don't mind my asking, of course."

"Actually, I do mind," I reply. "The FBI's work isn't something I can share with the public."

"But surely, the *mayor* of the town whose reputation you're tarnishing deserves to know something about the status of your investigation?" he snaps back.

Aha. His ego is bruised. Well, that's not something that can be helped. And his emotional reaction puts him on the defensive, which is to my advantage.

"Don't take it personally," I say cheerfully. "Sometimes criminal organizations prefer the cover of a peaceful small town to do their work. It can be easier to hide in plain sight. It has no bearing on your effectiveness as a mayor."

"I see," he murmurs. There's something vaguely menacing in his tone. Almost threatening.

"You grew up here," he says then. "Isn't that right?"

It sounds like a question, but it's clearly not.

"Yes, I did," I admit.

"Mmm. So did I." One corner of his mouth twitches. "Funny we never ran into each other back then."

"I don't think we're the same age," I observe.

"True. And also, I doubt we ran in the same circles."

The insult is clear. As is the implication underneath it. Mayor Holloway has had a look into my background. He knows about my childhood.

"You probably had reason not to like it here very much," he continues. "Living in that trailer park. And then foster care afterwards." Holloway makes a *tsk* sound with his mouth. "So sad when people fall through the cracks. I suppose it's understandable that you'd have a personal vendetta against the town."

This is not what I was expecting. I can't help it: I burst out laughing. "What?" I ask in disbelief.

"Though I must say it's fairly immature after all these years, to be so committed to hurting the good name of our town with unfounded rumors."

"I'm sorry to say, this is not a question of rumors, Mayor Holloway. We received a tip from a citizen, and it seems as though that tip may be credible."

The look on Holloway's face doesn't change. But as I watch, his skin goes from an even-toned pale pink to a blotchy red. "That's not possible," he bites out.

"Oh, it is," I assure him. A little late, I realize I might have said too much. But knowing I've hit a nerve with him is too satisfying for me to completely regret it.

"Ms. Brentano," he sneers, "I believe it's time for me to have a word with your supervisor. Your presence here in Tanner Springs is no longer welcome."

I shrug. "Special Agent Craig Lafontaine. Cleveland Field Office."

"I want you out of this town, Ms. Brentano."

"That's *Agent* Brentano," I correct him. "And I will be gone soon. Just as soon as I have the information I need."

Mayor Holloway doesn't bother to shake my hand as he leaves. He simply tugs his expensive suit coat into place, brushes past me, and heads toward the elevator.

I wait until the doors shut behind him before I snort and turn away. I guess I won this battle.

Still, I'd better be careful and keep my eyes open. I wouldn't be surprised if Holloway is spoiling for war.

* * *

When I tap on Natalia's door, a tiny, halting voice calls out, "*Come in.*"

I push into the room to find her sitting up in bed, looking much more cheerful than last time I saw her. In a chair beside her is a woman of about forty-five years old. She has brown hair flecked with gray, tied back in a loose ponytail. Her face is slightly weathered, and kind.

"Hello," she says in accented English. "Are you the FBI agent?"

"Olga?" I ask. At her nod, I reply, "Yes, I'm Brooke Brentano. Thank you so much for being here to help Natalia."

"It's my pleasure," she smiles. "I clean houses for a living, but I told my customers today, I am sick."

"That's very kind of you." I nod at Natalia. "How is she?"

"She is good!" Olga looks over at the girl. "I'm helping her with her English." Olga says something to Natalia, who looks at me with determination.

"Thank you for helping me," she recites. "I am very grateful."

"Oh, Natalia," I say. Tears spring to my eyes, but I manage to swallow them back down. "It's my pleasure."

"She knows some English," Olga explains. "But only from school. And from…" she trails off, her face stricken.

I nod quickly. "I understand." I glance around the room and spot a chair sitting in one corner. I pull it toward the bed next to Olga and sit down. "Natalia," I say, looking at Olga so she'll translate. "I am working on finding your father. When we find him, we will fly him here to come get you. And then together, you'll go home."

Olga speaks to Natalia, whose face blossoms into a wide smile. "Thank you," she whispers, her eyes overflowing with tears.

I have to clear my throat before I continue. "You're welcome," I say. "Before you go home, I would like to get an official statement from you. Which will probably take place in Cleveland. With an official interpreter. For now, though, I'd like to ask you some more questions about what happened to you, if that's okay?"

I wait for Olga to explain. When she's done, Natalia nods at me.

"Okay. Here goes."

I ask Natalia to repeat the story she told me yesterday, about how she got here, and how she escaped. She gives me a few more details this time, but her story is exactly the same as before. I take notes and ask for clarification here and there.

"Natalia," I say then, "I'd like to ask you about something that happened yesterday. After you talked on the blue phone to the interpreter, there was a man who came into the room. The man with the leather vest."

Natalia's eyes grow wide and frightened. She nods her head and says something to Olga.

"She says the man who came in yesterday was wearing the same vest as one of the men who would come to where she was being held. He was there often, and went with her and some of the other girls."

"How many men were there, Natalia? About how many men came to have sex with you and the others?"

Natalia answers through Olga. "More than a dozen."

"And how many girls were held with you?"

"Ten."

"The man in the leather vest," I press. "Are you *sure* this was the same vest that you saw on the man yesterday? Or just one that looked sort of like it?"

Natalia shakes her head and speaks rapidly to Olga. "The same. She says she recognizes the word from her English lessons back home because she heard some English prayers and knew that means 'God'."

"*Lord*," Natalia repeats emphatically.

I take a deep breath. This is a question I don't want to ask, but I have to. "Natalia. What did the man look like? The one who... *hurt* you... who was wearing that leather vest? I need you to describe him in as much detail as possible. Everything you can remember about him."

I let Natalia take her time, writing down notes as Olga translates. From what Natalia tells me, the man in the leather cut is on the older side, maybe her father's age, with gray and black hair and a gray beard. He's large, strong-looking but with a stomach. Natalia even describes a few of his tattoos. One in particular, on his left bicep, stood out to her. A skull with long hair and a bandana, pointing a gun in his skeletal fist.

Eventually, I see that Natalia is getting tired, and I remember that she's still recuperating from a terrible ordeal.

"Okay, I think that's enough," I say, smiling at the both of them. "Thank you so much, Natalia. I'm hoping to be back tomorrow with news about when your father will be here."

"When will she get out of hospital?" Olga asks me.

"I'm not sure," I say. "I'm going to go talk to the nurses about that. But we'll find her a place to stay, don't worry."

Natalia leans over and whispers something to her. Olga hesitates.

"Natalia says she is afraid to leave hospital. She is afraid they will come for her."

For some reason, Jarred Holloway's face flashes in my mind when Olga says this.

"I'm just here visiting a dear friend. Just a happy coincidence that I should run into you."

I never told Chief Crup I was investigating a human trafficking tip.

Somehow Holloway knew it, though.

I think back to the laundromat. And how it was closed the first time I was there.

And how the police car followed me around in the days after I visited Chief Crup.

My spine tingles at the back of my neck. Something's not right.

"Natalia," I say. "I'll come back and visit you again, very soon. In the meantime, don't worry. I'll keep you safe. I promise."

As I walk out of the hospital room, my mind is swirling in a million directions. After a few days of having essentially no leads, suddenly there are strands of them everywhere.

First, though, I go in search of Isabel. Thankfully, she's working this shift. I see her coming out of a patient's room near the nursing station.

She smiles, recognizing me instantly. "Agent…"

"Brooke," I interrupt her. "Isabel, I just came from Natalia's room. Can you tell me when she's being discharged?"

"Well," she begins. "Physically, except for being a little malnourished, there's nothing wrong with her. The hospital is going to want her out of here as soon as possible since she's not got insurance." She frowns regretfully. "I don't think we'll be able to keep her here beyond tomorrow."

"Okay." It's not ideal, but at least I know. "Look, I need to level with you. I'm a little worried that she could potentially be in some danger. I can't quite explain, but ideally, I'd like to have her room guarded. Unfortunately…" I hesitate. "I, um, would prefer not to involve the local police. And until I can get another agent down here to keep an eye on her, I don't have a lot of options."

Isabel snorts and rolls her eyes. "You don't have to apologize about not wanting the police involved. Remember, I'm with one of the Lords of Carnage. I know a lot more about the cops in this town than most. And trust me, under Mayor Holloway, they're the last people I'd call for protection."

I blink at her, surprised. It's no shock that the MC wouldn't trust cops, but it's interesting that she's mentioned Holloway as well. I take a deep breath and decide to take a leap of faith.

"I'll be back as soon as I can. I need to work on finding Natalia a safe place to be after she's released. In the meantime, is there any way that you can keep an eye on her? Make sure no one goes in there who shouldn't be?"

Isabel reaches out and puts a hand on my arm. "I'll tell the other nurses, and get hospital security to keep an eye on her room."

Relief floods through me. "Thank you so much, Isabel."

"Don't mention it. Really." Her eyes lock on mine. "I know what it's like to feel unsafe, and to need protection."

I walk out of the hospital feeling better than I have in days. But with every step, a weight begins to return, in some ways even heavier than before.

I just asked Isabel to trust me, and to help me. She agreed without reservation.

And now, she thinks I'm off to find Natalia a place to stay. Which I am.

But I'm also about to go spy on her husband's club.

And what I find might end up blowing the Lords of Carnage apart.

19
BEAST

As soon as we get back to Tanner Springs, Angel and I head straight for Rock's house. When we get there, Trudy greets us at the door.

"Jesus, I *just* got Rock home." She narrows her eyes at us. "Can't you men leave him the fuck alone for even a minute to let him recuperate?"

"This is important, Trudy," Angel tells her. "I'm sorry, darlin', but it can't be helped."

"All right," she sighs, and stands back from the door. "Come in. But wipe your goddamn feet. And don't stay long. I'm kickin' you out if you're still here in half an hour."

Rock is sitting on the living room couch, a couple of Trudy's throw pillows propped up around him. "Ah, geez, the welcome wagon," he mutters, but he looks glad to see us.

"I wish that was all we were here for." Angel takes a seat in an overstuffed chair next to the couch.

"What?" Rock looks from Angel to me. "Somethin' go wrong with the drop?"

"It was an ambush," Angel says without preamble.

"What the fuck are you talkin' about?" Rock demands, rising halfway off the couch. "That can't be right!"

"No doubt about it, Rock," I retort, my jaw tense. "Sarge and Horse are dead."

"Jesus Christ!" Rock explodes.

"It was a trap," Angel growls. "Whoever was supposed to meet us wasn't there. The Outlaw Sons came in their place." He waits a beat. "With some Iron Spiders."

Rock freezes. His face contorts into a mask of anger. "The Spiders," he repeats.

"We finished them all," Angel continues. "The ones that were there, anyway. But we only have a rough idea how many Outlaw Sons there are. And we have no idea how many Iron Spiders were left after we blew up their compound and killed their prez. Maybe all the ones that were left patched into the Sons. Maybe the ones that came for us wore their Spiders cuts to show us that this was revenge for what we did to them."

"So we're at war." His voice is quiet, but deadly.

Angel nods once. "The Outlaw Sons were never in this to do a deal with us. They were in it to *end* us." His eyes turn black and fierce. "This won't be over until one of our clubs is wiped out, Rock. Off the face of the earth."

Rock roars in fury, leaning forward and slamming his fist on the coffee table in front of him. Objects fly off the surface. He jumps up off the couch, kicking at the table and sending it careening into the wall opposite him.

"Jesus Christ!" Trudy shouts, running in from the kitchen. "Rock, what the hell is wrong with you? What have you two done to work him up like this?"

"Shut the fuck up, you cunt!" Rock yells, rounding. He raises a large, meaty fist as he strides toward her. "Get the *fuck* out of this room, now!"

"Rock!" Angel's up and shoving himself between them. "Come on, brother. Calm down." He reaches an arm back and gently pushes Trudy away. "Look, Trudy's right. You gotta calm down. You're no good to us if you're lyin' in a box."

Rock shoots Trudy a look of pure disgust. "Get outta here," he snarls.

She narrows her eyes at him. "Fuck you, Rock," she hisses. "Just fuck you."

Trudy storms out of the room. Rock clenches his teeth and turns back to the couch. "Shit. Sarge and Horse." He sits down, shaking his head. "Everyone else okay?"

I shake my head. "Bullet got shot. Smiley is patching him up."

"You get those motherfuckers?"

"The ones that were there, yeah. All dead." Angel's lip curls into an evil grin. "Ain't much left of their faces, though. The Sons are gonna have to identify 'em by their patches."

Rock stares into space. "The guns?" he finally says.

"We have them," Angel says. "I'm guessin' they thought they'd take our club out, and end up gettin' em back in the end."

"They ain't takin' this club out," Rock rasps. "I will fuckin' kill each and every one of 'em myself if I have to."

The three of us sit in silence for a few moments. This war that just started between us and the Outlaw Sons, it's gonna get big. It could pull in most of the clubs in eastern Ohio: us, them, our chapter to the south, the Death Devils… It ain't gonna be solved in a week, or even a month.

It's the outlaw equivalent of World War III.

We stay for a few more minutes and try to think of something to say to cheer Rock up, but the war with the Outlaw Sons is too much on all our minds. Trudy comes in twice more, and both times Rock shouts at her to get out, getting more and more agitated by the second. Eventually, we decide to take off before he has another heart attack.

"You stay away from here," Trudy orders us as we walk to the door. "He was in a foul mood anyway, before you came. He ain't gonna get better if you come here and keep riling him up."

"You okay, darlin'?" Angel asks. "He was a little rough on you back there."

"I can handle him," she grumbles, and then gives us a disgusted look. "But you two ain't makin' it any easier."

Trudy watches us for a few seconds as we walk down the sidewalk toward our bikes, then slams the front door behind us.

"You headin' back to the clubhouse?" I ask Angel.

"Eventually," he frowns. "I gotta call church. Talk to the club about the ambush and the war." Angel runs a hand roughly through his hair. "But I wanna talk to you first. And I'm fuckin' starving. Come on."

Twenty minutes later, we're sitting in a back booth at the Lion's Tap downtown, a couple glasses of draft in front of us.

"I gotta call Axel and tell him we're at war," Angel is saying. Axel's the president of the new chapter of the Lords of Carnage to the south. "They might not get hit right away, but they will eventually. They need to prepare. They need to know it's serious. That we've lost men."

"Speaking of which. We gotta notify Sarge and Horse's families," I reply. "And plan a memorial." Fuck, it makes me feel sick to say that. I can't believe they're gone.

"Yeah," he nods glumly. "Jesus, this is a hell of a time for Rock to be outta commission. It ain't good to be operating without a president right now."

"You'll hold us together, brother." I drain what's left of my beer and signal to the waitress for another. "Shit, you've been VP for a long time. You know what you're doin'. Ain't nobody in the club who doubts that for a minute."

Angel snorts. "Except Rock, maybe."

"Nah. He knows the club's in good hands. He just doesn't like it when he's not out in front, callin' the shots."

"Yeah. Well. That's one of the things I wanted to talk to you about." The waitress brings our food and moves away. Angel looks me in the eye. "I'm not so sure how soon he's gonna be back in the saddle. Trudy told me in the hospital that Rock's doc wants him to do a complete overhaul of his lifestyle. Diet, exercise, all that noise. And above all, no stress. Apparently his scans showed he'd had a couple mini heart attacks before this one, and there's a bunch of scarring and shit. I guess he's at risk for another attack, and his ticker can't take much more."

"Fuck," I whistle. "He ain't gonna take that very well."

"No shit. I don't expect him to take it at all. I tried to talk to him about it, but he blew up and said I was tryin' to take over his club."

"That's bullshit. He doesn't believe that."

"I dunno." Angel shrugs. "Wouldn't be the first time we've clashed when he thinks I'm challenging his authority. When I went to the hospital for the first time after his attack, he told me not to make any decisions about the club without consulting him first. Well, given the situation, I don't think that's gonna be possible. There's gonna be times I'm gonna have to decide shit quickly."

"He knows that," I say. "Or he will. The club'll back you up, brother."

"Rock's been like a father to me," Angel continues. "In a lot of ways, a hell of a lot more than my own father was. This club's my family."

Angel's father was Abe Abbott. He used to be the mayor of Tanner Springs. Used to be, that is, until he let greed and power get the best of him.

Abe Abbott and Rock had a long-standing gentlemen's agreement about the Lords of Carnage. An agreement that allowed both the mayor's office and the motorcycle club president to function in a kind of peaceful coexistence. The deal was, the Lords took care to keep their less legal business activities out of the spotlight, and the authorities of Tanner

Springs wouldn't look too hard at any of their comings and goings.

It was a deal that worked perfectly for everyone concerned, for many years. Until Abbott found himself in financial trouble and running up against an unexpectedly tough opponent in the mayoral election: Jarred Holloway. Abbott made a couple of very bad decisions, and ended up betraying the club's trust. Especially Rock's.

Some of the club members weren't too sure at the time whether Angel's loyalty to the Lords of Carnage would trump his allegiance to his own father. But Angel knew that Abe had fucked up, and badly. He stuck by the Lords and by his president. And any doubts the brothers might have had about him evaporated.

In the end, Abe Abbott went missing — either skipping town or meeting his end at the hands of the Iron Spiders, who he'd also been cutting deals with behind our backs. None of us knew where he was or what had happened to him. I sometimes wondered whether Angel knew anything about it, though I'd never ask him.

"The club's my family," Angel says again, pounding his fist softly on the table. "But so's Rock. I gotta do my best by both of them."

"You will, brother."

"We'll see." He eyes me. "But that's part of why I wanted to talk to you. I need you to tell me more about the situation with this fuckin' fed."

I nod. I figured this was where we were heading. "I pretty much told you everything I know. She's here investigating a tip her office got, about a trafficking ring operating out of this area. I ran into her at the Downtown Diner, and then again a couple days later. She eventually told me why she was here. And it just so happened that not long after that, Isabel mentions in passing that some girl from Ukraine came into the hospital with injuries, and she looked like she'd been held hostage or something. Turns out, once they get a translator in there, that she was being sold for sex. And when I came into the room and the girl saw my cut, she started freaking out, screaming and shit. And she's convinced one of the men who was fuckin' her was wearing this exact same cut."

"So this fed chick is gonna come knocking on our door." His jaw goes hard.

"I don't know. I've told her it couldn't be one of us, but I don't know if she believes it. I doubt it'll be enough for her not to follow up on it."

Angel eyes me. "You bangin' her?"

The question's so blunt it takes me by surprise.

"Yeah," I admit.

"Shit, son, where's your head at?" he growls.

"It ain't serious." It's true, but for some reason when I say it, I don't sound all that convinced. "Just some unfinished business from the past, is all."

"It's fuckin' stupid, is what it is. That's why the past is the past, brother. You don't drag it into the present." He shakes his head in disgust. "Now you're helpin' her in an investigation that's gonna lead her straight to us. Right when we got other shit to deal with."

"It ain't like that, brother. She's not gunnin' for the club. She's got other fish to fry."

But Angel's not convinced. "Can't trust the law, brother. Either they're crooked as shit, or they're on some sacred mission and think they're wearing white hats." He scoffs. "Either way is bad, but the white hats are worse. They have a price, same as everyone else. They just don't know it. At least the corrupt ones know they're corrupt."

In the end, against his better judgment I convince Angel to let me arrange a meeting between him and Brooke. So he can decide for himself what to make of her. I tell him I'll get in touch with her after he calls church.

Turns out, I don't have to wait that long.

20
BROOKE

After my visit to Natalia, I go to the county tax office. I ask one of the workers there to look up the property tax record of the E-Z Wash Express. She's friendly and helpful at first when I tell her who I am and what I'm looking for: A residential address and telephone number for the owner of the laundry. When she comes back to the counter after going back to consult the records, there's a strange look on her face.

"All I can give you is the name of the owner on record. That name is M.L. Stephanos," she says, handing me a stickie note.

"I know that already, though. I need to be able to contact Mister Stephanos."

"I'm sorry, that information isn't listed."

"Not listed? That doesn't sound right. There must be a mailing address to send the bills."

"The only address listed is the business itself."

Frustrated, I go from there to the laundromat itself, determined to get the information out of the old lady who works there. But strangely, when I pull into the lot, I see it's closed again, just like the first time I went there.

I'm sitting in my car, trying to decide what my next move should be, when my phone rings. I take it out and see that it's a Cleveland area code.

"Brentano," I answer.

"It's Lafontaine, Brentano," my boss says in his standard slightly impatient voice. "I'm calling for an update."

I'm surprised. He certainly hasn't seemed interested in this case up until now. I tell him about Natalia, happy to have something concrete to give him. Strangely, I find myself skipping over the detail about the motorcycle club cut, deciding I'll hold that information back until I can verify whether someone fitting her description of the man is one of the Lords of Carnage.

"Natalia's concerned about her safety," I conclude. "And frankly, I think there's some legitimacy to that concern. I'd like to put a security detail on her until we can get her out of the area, sir. I was actually planning to call you about that."

"Is there some reason you can't coordinate that with the local police department, Brentano?"

"Um…" I hesitate.

"The mayor down there gave me a call a little while ago, by the way," he tells me. "Says he's been more than willing to help you with your investigation, but you've turned down all offers from him."

So Holloway *did* call my boss. He sure didn't waste any time, that's for sure. "Actually, sir, that's not really the case. The mayor doesn't seem to appreciate my presence here in Tanner Springs. Trust me, he hasn't offered to help me."

"Well, he *has* offered that help to *me*. And frankly, Agent Brentano, I don't have unlimited resources to be sending down there, when there's law enforcement in place that's already willing to do the job. So you'll need to coordinate with them."

Like hell I will. "But sir…"

"That's all the chatting I have time for, Brentano. Unless you have more to report than just a girl who doesn't speak English and no way to substantiate her claims."

I hang up the phone, outraged and demoralized. I've always known Lafontaine doesn't like me much, but this feels like more than that. Like the investigation doesn't even matter to him. The victims don't even register to him. As long as I fuck up, he'll be happy. There's not a chance in hell he'll ever give me more resources to work with. Hell, if I showed him any success at all, he'd probably pull me off the case and assign someone else to it.

In some ways, I've never been a very good fit for the FBI. Oh, on paper there's nothing that would tell you this. Ever since I was eighteen, I had dreams of doing exactly what I'm doing right now. I worked my ass off to get in. And God, I was proud when I got my Letter of Appointment.

Why did I want it so badly? To prove something, I guess. Mostly to myself. Growing up, I never had people around me who expected me to amount to much. I was quiet in school. A decent student, but a little unkempt and unremarkable. My teachers mostly ignored me. Everyone just seemed to assume I wasn't going end up doing anything important.

I wanted to prove people wrong. I wanted to accomplish something hard. Something special. I wanted to prove I was someone.

I also wanted to be in the FBI because I thought it would be about getting justice for people who were hurt. I wanted to take down criminals who hurt the innocent.

I guess in my mind, it would be a little like the adult me getting justice for my younger self. Almost like being able to reach into the past and do something to protect the girl I once was, years after the fact.

This case should be a dream come true for me in that respect.

Now that I'm actually starting to get somewhere, I should be happy as hell.

But instead, I'm seeing that my fate is in the hands of someone who doesn't want to see me succeed.

And there's not a goddamn thing I can do about it.

I almost go back to the hotel to wallow in self-pity. But I have a job to do, even if Craig Lafontaine doesn't want me to do it.

I point my car in the direction of the Lords of Carnage clubhouse. When I pull into the lot, there are fewer motorcycles parked out front than I remember there being last time. I'm a little intimidated being here without Travis, but I'm hoping I can get in and find Jewel before anyone notices me and tells me to leave — or worse. Parking my car off to one side, I take a deep breath, then get out and stride purposefully toward the door before I can second-guess myself.

I'm in luck: one of the first people I see when I push inside is Jewel, who's wiping down some tables by the bar.

"Hey!" she greets me enthusiastically, but then her eyes flicker and she looks toward the door. "You here with Beast?"

"No," I tell her, and cross the room quickly to get to her. "Look, I know this is probably not allowed, but I came here to see you." *Among other things.* "Since I didn't know where you lived, I figured this was my best shot."

"Oh. Sure, that makes sense." She tucks the towel she was using into one of her belt loops. "What's up?"

"Um, could I get something to drink?" I ask, to buy some time. "I'm really thirsty. Just a club soda or a glass of water would be fine."

"Yeah, no problem. Come on." I follow her over to the bar and sit down at the same stool I used when I was here with Travis the last time. As Jewel grabs me a glass and fills it with soda water, I glance around the room at the smattering of men playing pool or observing a game. None of them come close to fitting the appearance of the man Natalia described.

Jewel sets the glass in front of me. "Here you go."

"Thanks," I say. I take a long drink, even though truthfully I'm not thirsty at all. "Oh, man, that tastes good," I sigh. "I was parched."

"So, what can I do for you?" she asks, leaning against the counter.

"Well, I have kind of a favor to ask you. And I feel bad asking it, since I barely know you, but I don't know what else to do."

"What is it?"

"Natalia is getting out of the hospital tomorrow," I begin. "She needs a place to stay for a few days, until we locate her father and he manages to come get her. She's afraid that the men she escaped from will be looking for her, and frankly, I don't think that's an unreasonable fear. I need to find somewhere where she'll be out of sight." I take a deep breath. "And I was wondering if you might be willing to take her in for a little bit."

"Of course," Jewel says without hesitation. "Olga and I can do it together. We live on the same floor of our apartment building. Natalia won't even have to go outside if she doesn't want to."

"Oh, my gosh, that would be great. I really appreciate this, Jewel." Relief spreads through me. Well, at least *one* of my problems is solved, albeit temporarily.

Jewel is assuring me it's no problem when the front door opens and a crowd of men starts flooding in. There are at least a dozen of them, and from the expressions on their faces, something bad either has happened or is about to.

I'm relieved to see that none of them fit Natalia's description.

The men over by the pool tables look over at the group streaming in. One of them, a tall, square-jawed and rugged man with anger flashing in his eyes, barks, "Church. *Now.*"

"Shit," Jewel murmurs as we both watch them stream past. She pulls the ponytail holder out of her hair and stares at the group as they head straight for a room toward the back. "Something's not right."

The square-jawed man looks around the room, his eyes landing on us. "Jewel," he half-yells, his eyes flashing. "Get your friend outta here. This ain't no place for a civilian to be right now."

"What the fuck are you doing here?" shouts a familiar voice behind me. I turn to see Travis, looking absolutely furious.

"I just came…" I begin, reddening at the thought that I'm going to have to lie to him. But he's having none of it.

"Get the hell out, Brooke," he says, grabbing me by the arm. "I mean it. This ain't the place or the time."

He pulls me out of the clubhouse by the elbow. Once we're out in the parking lot, he starts dragging me toward my car. "Go. Now."

"What's wrong?" as I stumble along.

"None of your business."

"But I need to talk to you, Travis!"

"Later," he barks.

"When?"

"When I'm fucking able to!" he shouts. "Go back to the hotel!" He turns on his heel and strides toward the clubhouse. "And don't come here again. You understand me?"

The door slams behind him. After a second, Jewel comes out, a cell phone in her hand.

"Hey," she murmurs. "Let's exchange cell numbers. You can call me as soon as you know when Natalia's being released. I'll talk to Olga when I go home tonight and figure out a plan."

I give her my number, and she texts me so I'll have hers. "Thanks."

"No worries." She glances back at the building. "And don't mind Beast. Something bad must have happened for the men to be acting like this. I'm sure it has nothing to do with you."

I hope she's right. But if Travis suspects I came here to look for Natalia's rapist, he'll have every reason to be furious at me. I just hope Jewel doesn't get in trouble for letting me stay.

21
BEAST

Church is fucking grim.

The men take Sarge and Horse's deaths hard. The thirst for blood is in the air. Outlaw Sons blood. Iron Spiders blood. The fact that we ended all the fuckers who ambushed us isn't enough. They want full-on annihilation.

Bullet's in the chapel with us, his wound patched up by Smiley. He's greeted as a hero.

Angel pounds the gavel to calm the angry shouting and the calls for revenge. "All right. This war the Sons started. We will end it. We will end *them.*" Shouts of approval greet his words. "But the Lords aren't gonna fight a bunch of fucked up street scuffles. When we're finished, the Outlaw Sons and what's left of the Spiders will be wiped off the face of the earth. But until that day comes, we plan. We make them sweat. We need to find out the full extent of their operations.

Where their compound is. Who they do business with. Where their weak links are." He looks down the table. "Tweak. You're in charge of intel. Recon. Tell me what resources you need, and you've got them."

Tweak nods. "You got it, boss."

There's a small ripple in the room. This is serious shit. And Angel's in charge. Rock's absence is felt, but Angel doesn't give us time to think about it.

"I'm gonna talk to Axel," he continues, referring to the president of our chapter to the south. "Tell him about everything. Let them know they need to watch their backs. And I'm gonna get in touch with Oz. Tell him we might need their help."

Oz is the president of the Death Devils, a club to our east. Our clubs have a solid alliance these days — not the least of which reason is his daughter Isabel is with our brother Thorn now.

"You think we need to go into lockdown?" Lug Nut asks.

"No. Not yet. I don't want the old ladies to be too alarmed." Angel scans all of our faces. "This is the new reality. Life during wartime ain't gonna be easy. We need to make sure it ain't any rougher on the families than it has to be."

We talk security, and Angel tells all of us to watch our backs and to not travel outside our territory without letting him know. He ends the meeting with a final, hard bang of the gavel. The men file out, silent and grave.

"Angel," I say to him as he stands. "I gotta talk to you."

"What is it?" He looks like he's aged five years in the last three hours.

"Brooke. The fed. That was the woman talking to Jewel when we came in."

"She was here?" he asks, incredulous.

"Yeah." I have to tell him the truth. "It ain't the first time, either. I brought her here a couple days ago."

"What the fuck is wrong with you?" Angel explodes. "I can't fuckin' believe this. Why?"

"Temporary insanity," I sigh.

I tell him it started out with me tryin' to help Brooke get the Ukrainian girl some second-hand clothes to wear for when she got out of the hospital. Jewel was the first person I thought of to ask. "I don't know that many chicks who don't dress like hookers," I grunt. "Thought Jewel might have some stuff. So, I introduced Brooke to her."

"And now the FBI agent you're fucking knows where our goddamn clubhouse is," he sneers.

I don't say anything. I royally fucked up, there's no getting around it. But at that moment, I wasn't seeing Brooke as a fed. I was just seeing her as… Brooke. The girl I knew so long ago. The woman whose tears I couldn't help but want to dry.

The woman whose bed I wanted to be in.

And now, shit's all fucked up. She's in my head all the time. And even though I know deep down she doesn't give a shit about what our club does, the fact remains that her investigation is getting her uncomfortably close to the Lords.

"I'm gonna go find her," I say. "I'm gonna get her to tell me what the fuck she was doing here today. But I think you need to talk to her. You and I both know our club ain't mixed up in the shit she's uncovering. But she needs to hear it from you."

"I ain't talkin' to no fed," Angel insists.

"I don't see as how you have a choice, brother." My jaw clenches as I look at him. "This is the only way to keep control of the situation. If she thinks we're hiding something, she's gonna go lookin' for it."

"Fuck," he groans. "Beast, what the fuck have you brought into the club?"

I don't say anything. Because damned if I know.

As Angel and I walk out of the chapel, there's a commotion outside. We go out into the main room to see

Rock standing in the middle of a group of our brothers, looking angry. About ten feet away is Trudy. She's crying, and shouting at him, shaking with rage.

She's wearing large dark glasses. But that can't hide the fact that her face is swollen and purpling. Her lower lip is busted.

"You're fucking *out* of my house!" she screams, flinging a set of keys at him. "Don't you come back again, ever! I'm changing the locks, and you will *never* touch me *again*!"

"Shit," Angel murmurs.

"Get out of my fucking way, all of you!" Trudy howls, turning on us. "You can keep this son of a bitch! He is a sick motherfucker, do you know that? And I have put up with his fucked up shit for the *last time*!"

The men standing near her clear a path as she grabs a chair and hurls it at Rock, narrowly missing him. Then she storms out of the clubhouse, still sobbing. After the door slams behind here, there's a moment of eerie silence.

"Fuck that gash," Rock growls. "She was more fuckin' trouble than she was worth. Good goddamn riddance."

I'm fuckin' stunned. I've heard Rock be sharp with Trudy before, but usually she gives as good as she gets. But I can't believe he was hittin' her. Only goddamn pussies hit women. I look around at some of the other brothers, who look as shocked as I am. Gunner and Thorn glance at each other and shake their heads.

"So, I'm back!" Rock bellows, raising his arms wide. "Your prez is back!"

In any other circumstance, the men would be yellin' and clappin'. But other than a couple of subdued whistles, the Lords don't say much.

If Rock notices anything is off, he doesn't show it. "We got a lot of shit on our plates, brothers. But first, it's time to party! I been cooped up for far too damn long. It's time to do something about it!"

He gets a few more claps and murmurs, but a lot of the guys just stand there.

"Come on! I need me some goddamn whiskey," Rock shouts. "And a goddamn hummer. Where the fuck are the club girls? Where's that young one? Bree, ain't that her name?"

Angel steps forward and puts his hand on Rock's shoulder. "Glad to see you back, prez," he says smoothly. "Look, how about we get you set up in your apartment first? I got a couple things I want to talk to you about."

Rock mutters something and angrily shrugs Angel's hand off, but he climbs the stairs to his apartment all the same. I feel some of the tension release in my shoulders.

"Jesus fuck," Thorn sighs next to me. "This is a hell of a development."

"Yeah." We should be happy to see Rock up and around, but this is some fucked up shit. He's likely to have another heart attack in the club, goin' on like this. And the way he's acting right now makes me less than thrilled to have him at the helm at the beginning of this war with the Outlaw Sons.

I need to go talk to Brooke. I want her to meet with Angel soon. We need to get that situation resolved, so we can focus on all the other shit going down right now.

I leave the clubhouse on my bike. The engine roars as I speed through the streets to Brooke's hotel. When I get there, I don't wait for the elevator. I go to the stairwell instead and take the steps two at a time. I push the fire door open and go into the brightly lit hallway with its swirling pattern of red-orange carpet.

There's no one in the hall besides me, but through the quiet I hear some noises coming from one of the rooms at the other end of the hall. It almost sounds like someone's throwing around furniture or something.

Then, I hear a woman scream.

And I realize it's Brooke.

22
BROOKE

On the way back to the hotel to wait for Travis, I realize I need to grab something for dinner. I'm hardly in the mood to go to a restaurant, but I don't have a kitchen and I'm sick of fast food. So, I choose a nondescript chain restaurant I saw on the highway about a mile from my hotel. I go inside, get seated, and order a dinner of high carbs and comfort food. When it comes, I sit and stare into space, eating mechanically and mulling over the situation.

I decide that when Travis comes to see me, I have to tell him the truth: that I went to the club to ask Jewel to help me with Natalia, yes. But that I also went there to scout for her alleged rapist.

I'm hoping he'll be less mad at me when I tell him I didn't see anyone who fit her description. But I'm not counting on it.

I'm not quite sure how I feel about that, myself. On the one hand, I'm incredibly relieved. I can't imagine how complicated and horrible it would be to find out that someone in his club really is involved in the ring that kidnapped Natalia. Or worse, that Travis's whole club is implicated in it, and he's been lying to me.

But on the other hand, that detail is one of the only leads I actually have.

I sum up all the pieces of information I have about this case in my head.

Natalia.

The laundromat, with almost no customers.

M.L. Stephanos.

The sparkly ring I found in the laundry's strangely empty basement.

The ring.

It's still sitting there on the small desk in my hotel room.

I should bring the ring to Natalia. Ask her whether she's ever seen it before.

It's an awfully long shot, I know. A thought born of desperation. But it's all I have.

I look down at my plate. I've been shoveling food in my face without paying much attention to what it tastes like or how much I've been eating, but I've only managed to finish about half of it. Suddenly, I can't eat another bite. I ask for the bill, throw a credit card at it, and drive the final mile to my hotel.

Instead of parking in my usual spot by the side entrance, I choose a place close to the front. I trudge inside and take the elevator, feeling disheartened and hoping that tomorrow will bring me better luck.

At my room, I slide my key card through the slot and open the door. Even though the sun hasn't set outside yet, the room is pitch black. I realize the maid must have shut the curtains, and reach in to fumble for the light switch.

Just as my fingers slide over the plastic plate, a hand grabs me by the wrist, pulling me roughly inside.

A strangled cry rips from my throat as my hip bone slams against the door handle. I hear the fabric catch and tear. Frantically, I grab for the door frame with my other hand, clawing at it to get purchase, but the door itself closes on my fingers and I have to wrench them away as the wood rips at my knuckles. Then I'm in free fall, my feet dragging across the floor as I try to get them under me.

Strong arms wrap around my waist, pulling me up and pinning me to my attacker. I kick out behind me, blindly, trying to connect with a knee or a shin. I manage to land a blow somewhere on his lower leg, and the pain causes him to let go of me just enough that I can plant one foot on the ground. Shouting, I grab one fist in the other and ram backwards into his solar plexus, then wrench my arm from his, corkscrew-style. He lets out a low roar. I spring free from his grasp and spin in place, lashing out blindly with my right hand in a claw. I manage to connect with his face, and feel the scrape as I dig gashes deep as I can into his cheek. I pull away before he can reach for me, and move behind where I think the far bed is.

The room is totally dark now that the door is closed. Squinting, I pray for my eyes to adjust enough that I'll be able to see something from the sliver of light coming in from underneath the door.

"You're fucking dead, you cunt," the man's angry voice hisses.

"I don't fucking think so," I spit back, reaching for the gun in my shoulder holster.

It's a stupid move. I realize too late that he was using my voice to locate me. A fist comes out of nowhere, connecting with my temple hard enough that I see stars. I shout in pain and reach my arms up to deflect the next blow. A slam sounds somewhere down the hall, and I scream as loudly as I can. The man spits out a curse, and then the door opens and he's out of the room and running down the hall.

I pull out my Smith and Wesson and bolt into the hallway, but the man has already pushed through the door into the stairwell. As I dash after him, a voice yells out behind me.

"Brooke!" calls Travis from the other end of the hall.

"He's getting away!" I yell, and sprint into the stairwell. I pound down the stairs as fast as I can with my head still ringing. I hear the echoes of my assailant's footsteps below me at first, but by the time I get outside, he's nowhere to be found.

I'm standing outside, panting, when Travis comes up behind me.

"Who was that?" he asks. When I look up at him, his face goes dark. "Did that son of a bitch do that to you?"

I reach up gingerly to feel the side of my face. The skin is already bruising and tender. "Yeah."

"You get a good look at him?"

I shake my head. "Not even a little bit."

Travis swears softly. "Come on. Let's get you back upstairs."

"I don't have my key card. I must have dropped it in the room."

"Okay."

He takes me by the arm and walks me gently toward the front entrance, where I tell the desk worker I've locked myself out. Thankfully, she recognizes me and doesn't give me any hassle. She does stare a little at my developing black eye, though, and gives Travis a quick reproachful glance.

When we're back upstairs, Travis takes the key card from me and goes in first. He flips on the light switch and looks around, checking in the bathroom. I follow behind him. It's strange to look at the room and see signs of our struggle in the dark. There's a chair overturned, and the covers on one of the beds have been pulled nearly off. I don't remember any of that.

"Come here," Travis says, leading me to the untouched bed. "You want some ice?"

"Later."

"You sure? That's gonna be ugly tomorrow."

I wince, not so much at the pain as at the fact that he just basically said I look like hell. Or that I'm *about* to look like hell, anyway.

"I'll grab a washcloth and put some cold water on it," I say, getting up.

"You think that guy has something to do with this trafficking thing?" he calls as I run the water.

I come back out, washcloth to temple. "I can only assume. I must be closer than I thought. Funny, it sure doesn't seem like it."

"Fuck," Travis swears, his face stormy. "Wish I'd gotten here five minutes sooner. I could use a punching bag tonight."

"Things not going to well with the club?" I ask.

He snorts. "You could say that."

"Want to talk about it?"

At this, Travis bursts out laughing. "Trust me, B, you do not want me to tell you any more."

Even though things feel pretty dismal right now, it feels good to hear him laugh.

"I thought you were mad at me," I remark. "For coming to the club."

"I am."

"Oh."

He leans closer and peers at my face.

"Take off the washcloth," he commands. I do as he says. "Yeah. That's not good."

"Do you suppose you could stop telling me how terrible I look?" I complain.

"You don't look terrible, B. You look good." His tone shifts down a register. "You always look good."

You do, too, I want to say.

Now that the immediate danger has passed, having him here — so uncomfortably close — is giving me *ideas.*

"That eye hurt much?" he asks gruffly.

"It's okay," I shrug.

"Yeah?" A corner of his mouth lifts. "Playing the tough chick. You always did play the tough chick, B."

It's disconcerting, having him call me that. Like he always used to. It makes my heart feel kind of soft and melty. I fight against it.

"I don't play the tough chick," I huff softly. "I *am* the tough chick."

Travis chuckles. "Yeah," he nods, leaning closer. "You are."

I'm about to ask whether he's making fun of me when he pulls me to him. My breathing speeds up as his mouth comes down on mine, and instantly I'm on fire, all thoughts of my blackening eye forgotten. His tongue brushes against my lower lip, and it sends a jolt of heat straight to my core. I moan into his mouth, surrendering to the pleasure.

Travis breaks the kiss and begins to trail his lips down my neck.

"This doesn't seem like 'mad'," I gasp.

"I can compartmentalize," he mutters.

"Does that mean you're gonna yell at me later?"

"Maybe." He tosses me back, onto the bed. "Now shut up."

Travis moves over me, his huge frame covering mine. Already, I feel the wetness building between my legs at the memory of the last time we did this. All thoughts of the last couple of hours evaporate, just like that.

"You've been thinking about this," he says as he reaches down, sliding his hand under my shirt. My body shivers at his touch.

"Yes," I breathe. There's no use in lying. I want him to know how much I want it. My eyes start to flutter closed.

Then: "Oh, shit."

"What?" I ask, startled. Then I realize what he's talking about.

"Sorry," I mutter, pulling away and standing. "Let me just take this off."

I take off my jacket and slide the straps of the shoulder holster off. Travis watches me, smirking.

"What?" I ask.

"Hot," he murmurs with a sexy half-grin.

Like an idiot, it sends shivers up my spine.

I set the gun and holster on the desk and move back to the bed. Travis pulls me down. "Where were we?"

Hardly believing my boldness, I reach for his hand and slide it under my shirt. "Here, I think."

"Good memory, B," he rasps. "Tell me, what do you do when you think about me?" Travis demands as his hand moves further up to cup my breast.

"What?"

"What do you do?" With his thumb, he begins to tease my nipple through my bra. "Do you touch yourself? Do you make yourself come?"

I suck in a breath and try not to moan. "Yes," I whisper, thinking about what I did last night in the shower before bed.

He lets out a low groan and shifts on the bed. "What do you think about when you touch yourself?" He slips my shirt over my head. I hear the slight click as he unclasps my bra.

"I…" His mouth is on my nipple, and I cry out, reaching up to thread my fingers in his hair. "Oh, God, Travis. Yes."

"Tell me what you think about." His whiskers are rough against my sensitive skin.

"This… Oh, my God. I think…" My breathing is ragged. "I think about you… about what you did to me last time.

About how you made me come with your tongue. And then how you filled me up. And…" I make myself say it. "I think about having you in my mouth."

"Fuck," he rasps. He grabs my hand. Pulling it toward him, he presses my palm against the throbbing heat of him. "Feel what you do to me, B."

I love that I make him like this. I love that he wants me. But I need to see more of him. I want more of his skin pressed against mine. A little frantically, I reach for the button of his jeans, and try to undo it. He rises from the bed and pulls off first his cut, then his shirt. Kicking off his boots, he gets rid of his jeans, until he's standing in front of me. I take a long moment to look, stopping to gaze at the raw beauty of his tattoos, and how they accentuate the angles of his body. The beast on his left pec stares at me, flame in its eyes.

Then, before he can stop me, I move down to the ground. Kneeling in front of him, I take him in my mouth.

He's too large for me to take very much of him in, but I do my best. My lips wrap around his head, my tongue sliding against the silken skin of his shaft. Travis lets out a low groan and freezes. One hand reaches down and strokes my cheek as I begin to slowly bob. I make love to his cock, exactly like I've done more than once in the fantasies I've had about him since I came back to town. I taste his heat, his desire, and I want more. I want to make him come like this. I want to be the one that does that for him.

"I know what you're thinkin'," he says tightly as I continue to stroke. "I'm not lettin' you finish me off like that, B. Not tonight. I need to be buried deep inside you when I come tonight, babe. I need to feel your pussy as it comes all around me." He fists his hand in my hair and gently pulls me off him, ignoring my mewl of protest.

"Take off your pants," he rasps. "And spread your legs. Wide."

I do as I'm told. I get down on the bed and look up at him. His cock is still glistening from my mouth.

"I've been thinkin' about how good you taste ever since last time," he murmurs, as he reaches up to slowly stroke himself. "And how hard you came when I fucked you with my tongue."

He takes a step closer. "This time, I told myself I was gonna torture you. Make you wait for it. Make you beg." My back arches, almost as though he's already touching me. "But I've got a different kind of torture in mind right now."

Before I can ask him what he means, he's grabbed my legs and pulled me to the edge of the bed. He slides the head of his shaft between my slick folds. I gasp and clutch at the bedcovers, begging silently for him to give me what I so desperately crave. I tense up, my legs falling further apart in spite of myself, as I angle toward him and thrust. Travis chuckles and pulls back, leaving me naked and exposed.

"Travis," I whisper. The throbbing between my legs is insistent, almost unbearable. "Please."

"Oh, don't worry, darlin'," he murmurs, lowering his head between my legs. "You're gonna get what you need."

Then his mouth is on me. His lips massage and suck, his tongue lashing and stroking, fast and deep. His hands grip my thighs and he pulls me into him, harder, as he devours me. His tongue slides over me, and I arch toward him and cry out as he drinks me like I'm sweet, like I'm honey and he can't get enough. I'm so close already that it doesn't take me long before his assault on my most sensitive spot pushes me over the edge and I shatter, calling his name. But even then, he doesn't let up, just grows more insistent as his strokes slide downward and deeper, becoming more rhythmic. I try to push him away but then even though I think it's too much, eventually the pleasure overtakes the pain as he licks me harder, faster, coaxing my body forward as all my muscles start to tremble at his touch.

Then all at once, another orgasm bursts from me, sudden and sharp as a whip. My throat is hoarse from the noises he's pulling from me, from shouting his name and begging him, and I no longer know whether I'm begging him to stop or to keep going, but he doesn't stop, his tongue keeps torturing me, and I'm so sensitive every single stroke sends my nerve endings into overdrive. I can't fight it, I need the release he's building for me, it's so good, he's finding the pleasure from so deep inside me I've never known anything like it, and orgasm after orgasm rolls through me, until I'm exhausted and weak, too exhausted to cry out or ask for mercy.

Finally, when I think I can't take any more, Travis moves over me and flips me onto my stomach, then pulls me up onto all fours. Standing at the edge of the bed, he grips my hips one more time and drives into me. The mass and heat of him fill me, and I feel myself tightening around him. One hand leaves my hip and fists in my hair, tugging my head back.

"I like to hear you beg, B," he rasps against my neck. Then he draws back and thrusts himself inside me to the hilt, before withdrawing and plunging again. I push back against him as he gives me thrust after thrust, each time deeper than the last. I physically feel him getting bigger as he gets closer to the edge. I know he's going to explode inside me soon, coat my insides with his heat, and the thought makes me gasp and thrust back against him even more. Then, with a roar, he plunges inside me once more and releases, filling every inch of me as he comes long and hard.

Travis kisses my back, the softness of his lips contrasting with the roughness of his beard.

"I don't want you to stay at the hotel tonight," he tells me.

"I'll change rooms," I say. "It'll be okay."

"Negative. You're coming home with me. And tomorrow we're gonna go talk to my vice-prez."

"What?" I look back at him, trying to read his face.

"You need to let go of this Natalia shit, Brooke. Our club doesn't have anything to do with it. And the Lords have got a world of other problems to deal with right now. We don't have the fuckin' patience for an FBI witch hunt. It's a distraction for both of us. And neither of us needs it right now."

"But…"

"Don't argue," he cuts me off. Travis stands up from the bed and reaches for his jeans. "Just get your bag and come on."

I pack light, and I tend to live out of my suitcase when I travel, so it doesn't take me long to grab my stuff.

"I'm not riding on the back of your bike with this," I tell him when I'm ready, pointing at my bag.

"Of course not," he scoffs. "Follow behind me in your car."

I can see him keeping an eye on my vehicle in his side mirror the whole way there. It should bug me that he's being so overprotective, but I have to admit it actually feels kind of good.

We pull up to an up-down duplex on a quiet street on the north side of town. Travis parks his bike, then comes to the car and grabs my bag, which he carries up the walk for me. He puts a key in the lock of one of the two front doors and nods me through to go up the stairs to the second floor.

"Who lives downstairs?" I ask as I climb.

"Landlord," he grunts. "He likes me because I'm not home much. And because I know how to fix his piece of shit car."

Upstairs, I push the door open into a sparsely decorated apartment with sloped ceilings. Travis carries my bag through a short hallway and into a largish bedroom.

"Bathroom's through there," he says pointing. "You need anything, just ask."

For a second, I think he's gonna have me sleep in here while he sleeps on the couch or something crazy like that. But then he pulls me into his arms.

"How you feelin'?" he asks. "That bump on your head any better?"

"To tell you the truth, I forgot all about it," I admit, reaching up to touch my cheekbone. "How does it look?"

"Like hell," Travis says with a grin. "But it'll heal."

I try and fail to stifle a yawn. "I guess this day has taken a lot out of me," I confess. Travis shoots me a suggestive leer. "Oh, stop it," I laugh, play-swatting at him.

He snorts. "Come on into the kitchen. I'm gonna give you a shot of bourbon to help you sleep. And then we're going to bed. I'm beat, too."

I'm too tired to argue with him, so I let him dose me with the bourbon and then climb into his king-size bed next to him. Travis pulls me close to him.

Within minutes, I'm fast asleep.

23
BEAST

If I was fucking up before by bringing Brooke to the club, I'm fucking up even more by bringing her to my place.

But I can't do otherwise. I wasn't about to leave her at the hotel.

I'm too keyed up to sleep after everything that's happened tonight. Brooke's out like a light, though. I sit in the dark and think instead. And find myself watching her as she sleeps.

I still remember how fucking angry I was when she left Tanner Springs. And when she literally ran into me at the diner that day, the fury that I thought had disappeared over the years came roaring right back. It was like the wound had been ripped back open, the scar tissue tearing clean through to the flesh underneath.

Now? I don't know what the fuck I think.

In a way, she's the last person I should even be giving the time of day. A fucking federal agent, for Christ's sake. Angel should kick my ass for even talking to her, much less bringing her around the club.

But I know Brooke. I know who she is, deep down. And the shit she's investigating is legit. Whoever these fuckers are, they deserve to rot in prison. I *want* her to get them. I want her to succeed.

And I want to make sure she doesn't get killed doing it.

I snort softly as I look down at her. I know if I said that out loud, she'd be pissed. She'd tell me she can take care of her damn self, thank you very much. Which I'm sure she can. You don't get into the FBI by bein' a cream puff.

But old habits die hard. And there was a time when I wanted to protect Brooke from everything bad in the world. I thought I could do it, too. And I thought she wanted me to.

Turned out, I was wrong. She didn't need me. Not at all. And I guess that was what hurt most of all.

I remember when I heard through the grapevine that Brooke's mom had died. We didn't really know each other at that point, but I'd watch her sometimes in the halls when she didn't think I was looking. I was getting laid pretty regularly at that point, so I wasn't really paying a lot of attention to the shy-looking girl with the wild blond hair and the nineties grunge style. But I definitely noticed her.

I didn't know she didn't have a dad when I heard her mom had passed away unexpectedly. I didn't really know anything about her situation.

Then one day after school, I came out of the exit by the parking lot and saw her sitting there, by herself. Looking like she was waiting for someone to pick her up but they hadn't shown.

Before I even knew I was gonna do it, I asked her if she wanted a ride. She gave me a look I couldn't quite read, and I thought she was going to turn me down. But then — just as I was gonna turn away — she shrugged and said yes. I still remember how she looked as she picked up her backpack and fell into pace beside me.

She didn't say much for the first couple of minutes. But then I made some joke or other that made her laugh. She threw back her head, and her tumble of blond hair cascaded down her shoulders, highlighted against the red plaid of her flannel shirt. I remember thinking how fucking gorgeous she was. Like I could've looked at that face for hours and not gotten sick of it. She liked the song that was playing through the speakers — Wasteland, by Ten Years — so I turned it up, and she started nodding her head to it and humming along.

When I dropped her off, I offered to give her a ride home whenever she wanted. And then the next day, I found myself hanging out by her locker after school, hoping to catch her. When her eyes met mine in the locker, she gave me a little smile.

So began our friendship. And then, little by little, a lot more than that.

I knew she hated being in the foster home they placed her in after her mom's death. She didn't give me a lot of specifics, but I knew it wasn't good. I always suspected there were things going on that maybe she wasn't telling me. But I never wanted to push Brooke further than she wanted to go. She had this tough streak to her, but underneath she was soft. I wanted to get to that soft place. And I was willing to wait.

I remember the first time I kissed her. Brooke fucking *trembled.* Shit, the girls I was used to, some of 'em would pretend to be virgins, but it was all just an act so they could play hard to get for a little bit. Brooke was different. That first kiss, I knew she wanted it, but I also knew I had to go slow. I knew from bein' in locker rooms and from what other girls said that I was bigger than average — much bigger — and I didn't want to scare Brooke. I wanted her to be ready for me, and for what I was sure would be her first time.

There was something about waiting that was actually kind of a turn-on. Oh, it was torture, don't get me wrong. I spent more time jacking off than you could imagine, just to keep the blue balls away. But I was makin' progress with her. When I'd take her out to a movie or just to go hang out, more often than not we'd end up dry humping in the back of my dad's truck or on a secluded picnic table in a city park. I got to know the way her breathing would speed up when I did something she liked. But I also learned that little hitch in her throat when shit was getting too intense and I needed to back off.

Then one day, she stopped talking to me.

We didn't have a fight. There wasn't anything that happened. She just totally fuckin' withdrew. I went to her locker after school, and she wasn't there. I looked around, but she was nowhere to be found. I drove to her house, but her foster parents said she wasn't at home.

For the next two days, she managed to completely avoid me at school, even though I knew her schedule like the back of my goddamn hand. Then, on the third day, I caught her coming out of a math class. I confronted her, but she looked through me like I was a total stranger. All the light that used to be in her eyes when she looked at me was gone. Her mouth was pursed, her jaw set. She totally froze me out.

At first, my ego was so fuckin' bruised I pretended I didn't care. I acted like she'd never mattered to me, even though nothing could have been further from the truth. I made sure she saw me hanging out in the halls, laughing with my friends. Girls always flirted with me, and I played it up, hoping she'd see it and get jealous.

Then, three weeks later, it was her eighteenth birthday. It was a school day, but she didn't show up. I looked for her all day, breaking my promise to myself to pretend like she didn't exist.

Finally that night, I couldn't take it anymore. I drove to her house, hoping to catch her by surprise. I thought maybe I could convince her to let me take her out to celebrate or something.

Her foster dad Mr. Bonner answered the door, looking pissed. He said she'd run away that morning, before they'd woken up. Left a note saying she wouldn't be back.

She skipped town. Without a trace.

I figured I'd never see her again.

I look down at Brooke now, watching her slow, even breaths. Her eyelids flutter like she's dreaming.

It feels good that she's let her guard down with me as much as she has. The way she loses herself in the moment when I'm fucking her — it's hotter than hell. She seems to need that, the loss of control.

My cock stirs under the sheets. I think about waking her up, but she needs her sleep.

Goddamnit.

I'm falling for a girl who already left me once.

What's that thing they say about the definition of insanity? Doin' the same thing over and over again and expecting a different result?

I must be about as insane as they come.

The next morning I let her sleep late. She wanders out of my bedroom around ten, wearing nothing but one of my T-shirts and lookin' so sexy it makes me want to stop what I'm doing and pull her back into bed.

"Why didn't you wake me up?" she complains groggily.

"You needed it. How's your head?"

"Not bad. How's it look?" She turns her face to show me. There's a purplish-green bruise blooming right where her cheekbone is, but the swelling's gone down.

"It's better today." I nod toward the kitchen. "There's coffee if you want it."

She shakes her head. "You have any bread for toast?"

"Yup. Help yourself. Hey, Jewel called. Natalia's already at her place. She got out of the hospital this morning. Isabel knew she was being discharged, so she called Jewel to come pick her up."

"Holy crap." Brooke shoots me a worried look. "I hope Jewel wasn't followed. After last night, I'm worried for Natalia's safety."

I see her point. "You think they need protection?"

"Maybe." She bites her lip. "Could we go over there? Like, now? I'd feel better seeing where Jewel lives for myself."

"Sure, we can do that."

"I'm going to take a quick shower." Brooke does an about face and heads for my bathroom. As she goes, she pulls my shirt up over her head, revealing that she's naked beneath it.

"You're killing me here," I call after her.

"Nothing saying you can't join me," she calls back, a smile in her voice.

Well, fuck.

That shower is barely big enough for me.

But goddamn if we won't make it work.

24
BROOKE

I tell myself that seducing Travis into the shower with me was just a fun stress reliever before what could be a very stressful day. But if I'm honest, I just want to prolong the feeling I've had with him since we got here last night.

The feeling of being safe. And secluded. Like there's only us, and the rest of the world doesn't matter.

Kind of fucked up, since we're not a couple. And this is only sex.

For him, at least. For me, I'm a little scared that it's starting to feel like something else. Something more.

When Lafontaine sent me down here to Tanner Springs, I had a lot of reservations about the whole thing. I wanted to do my job, but I didn't want the memories that I knew would come with returning to the town where I grew up. I resolved to keep my emotions at bay, and stay as uninvolved and unemotional as possible.

Instead, I ran straight into my past. And the first boy I ever loved. The only one, actually.

Because I *was* in love with Travis. He was the first person in my life other than my mom to make me feel special. Beautiful. Worth something.

It was the most amazing feeling when he used to look into my eyes. I couldn't figure out what he saw in me, but I couldn't get enough of it. Or of the way I felt when I was with him.

Except that underneath the warmth — underneath the wonder that someone would rather be with you than anyone else — there was something deeper. Darker.

Fear.

A fear so complicated I couldn't quite define it. I was afraid of how strong my feelings were for Travis. But it was more than that. I was afraid that the more I let him in, the more he'd see I wasn't as special or as beautiful as he thought I was. I was afraid if I told him about how my stepfather used to touch me sometimes when he was drunk, he'd think there was something wrong with me. I thought if I told him the look in Mr. Bonner's eyes told me he was thinking the same things, maybe Travis would think it was somehow my fault. That maybe I was asking for it. Leading them on.

And most of all?

I was terrified that if I let go — let myself trust Travis completely — he might turn out to be just like those men. An animal. A violent beast, hiding in plain sight in the shape of a man.

I wanted Travis so badly. I wanted more than anything to give myself to him. I loved the way he made my body feel, even though it scared me, too. I wanted more. I wanted *everything* with him.

Maybe we could have had it, too.

But then one day, shortly before my eighteenth birthday, I came back to the Bonners' after school. I thought I was alone in the house, but Mr. Bonner wasn't at work like I expected him to be.

He raped me on the landing of the stairs to the second floor. I didn't even have time to run up to my room and lock the door.

When Mrs. Bonner came home, I thought about telling her. I thought about running away that night. I thought about all sorts of things. But in the end, I didn't do any of them. Because somehow I knew Mrs. Bonner wouldn't believe me. And I didn't want CPS to place me in yet another home, where maybe things would be even worse.

So, instead, I said nothing. I stayed in my room, with my dresser up against my door, and waited for morning to come. I left for school. I walked the whole three miles there. I pretended nothing had happened at all.

Except that when I got close to the school grounds and thought about seeing Travis, I threw up behind a bush.

I couldn't see him. I couldn't stand the thought of him looking at me. I was sure he'd be able to see what had happened if he looked into my eyes. He'd know that I was dirty. If he touched me, I was sure I'd shatter into a million pieces.

I ran in the other direction. I spent the day walking around town, hiding from people so that no one would ask me why I wasn't in school. I only went back to the Bonners' that night because I didn't have any place else to stay. But I made sure Mrs. Bonner was there, and I barricaded my door with the dresser again.

The next day, I knew I couldn't avoid school again without getting myself into trouble, so I went. I managed to avoid Travis completely that day. But the following day he caught me outside one of my classes. He kept asking me what was wrong, but I couldn't tell him. I couldn't say anything. He thought I was mad at him, and that seemed like the best excuse, so I let him think it. I acted like he'd done something terrible. I pretended it in my mind, too. Pretended it until I almost believed it. Because I couldn't let Travis in. If I let him in — if I told him what had happened — I knew that everything I was afraid of with him would come true. He'd think I was disgusting. He'd look at me like I was damaged goods. And worst of all, maybe he'd think that he had a right to take what he wanted from me, whether I wanted him to or not.

Just like Mr. Bonner had.

On the morning of my eighteenth birthday, I left. I had a little money that got me out of town. I stayed in a homeless shelter in the city for a couple weeks, until I could get the death benefit from my mom's insurance policy. I got my GED, and used the insurance payout to pay for my first couple years of college. Student loans got me through the rest. I never looked back at Tanner Springs, or the Bonners.

Or Travis.

I know better now. At least in theory. I know I wasn't dirty. I know what happened to me wasn't my fault.

But I also know things couldn't have gone any further with Travis back then. If I'd stayed, I would have just saddled him with someone who was too fucked up to be any good as a girlfriend. I wanted him to be my first, but that was taken away from me. From us. I couldn't believe in a happily ever after, after that. I would have been waiting for things to go bad between us. I would have been waiting for Travis to show me he was just like the others.

And now, I know there's no way for things to ever be the same again between us. You can't change the past.

That's why it's crazy that I let myself get into this… *whatever* it is with him.

I should never have let Travis back into my life. For either of our sakes. I know he's trying to help me with this case, even though it puts him at risk with his club. But I don't know why.

It feels so good being with him again. Too good. I should be strong enough to stay away from him. I was strong enough once before — strong enough to leave him, even though it almost broke me.

The cold fact of the matter is there's no future for us. It's ridiculous to even hope. We're on opposite sides of the law, he and I. Even though my side isn't quite as squeaky clean as I wish it was.

I've never been more in doubt of the decisions I've made. Of this life I've chosen. I'm a mess, inside and out.

And Travis has turned into a Beast. Literally.

If I believed in signs from the universe, this one couldn't be more clear.

But the universe has screwed me over before. And right now, my heart is telling me to ignore my head. That sometimes a Beast is more of a man than all the rest.

* * *

After a quick breakfast, Travis takes me on his bike to visit Natalia. When we get to Jewel's place, she lets us into the small entry of her apartment. I stop Travis just inside the door.

"Maybe you should take your cut off," I suggest, remembering what happened last time Natalia saw it.

He looks down at the leather. "Good point," he says, shrugging it off.

Natalia is in Jewel's tiny living room, sitting on the couch. Olga is there, too, which is a relief. Natalia's wearing a pair of comfy sweats and a purple top with sparkles on it. She looks for all the world like any typical teenager. Fortunately, Natalia doesn't seem to recognize Travis as the man with the Lords of Carnage cut at the hospital. She gives us a wide smile and stands up to greet us.

"Hello, Brooke!" she beams. "I am so happy today!"

My heart swells as she comes up and gives me a big hug. It's a little hard to swallow for a second as I think about the hell that Natalia has escaped, and everything she's been through to get here.

And then I remember that if she's correct, there are at least nine other girls out there who are still in that hell.

"Thank you both so much for helping Natalia," I say to Jewel and Olga.

"It is our pleasure," Olga replies, waving a hand.

"Have you gotten any word about Natalia's father?" Jewel asks me.

"I'm planning to call my contact at the embassy today." I glance at Olga, and she translates for Natalia, who looks at me with hope. "I'll call or come back as soon as I have an update. In the meantime, is there anything I can do for you? Anything you need?"

Jewel chews her lip. "I know Natalia's still worried that the men will come for her. Now that we're out of the hospital, I suppose she's safer, but…"

Travis cuts in. "I'm gonna ask Angel to send some of the Lords here to keep an eye on things." He glances at Natalia. "Just to hang around outside the entrances of the apartment. Make sure no one gets in or out without their knowledge."

I thank him with my eyes, grateful that he realizes their presence in the apartment would make Natalia nervous.

"Are you sure?" Jewel asks doubtfully. "It's not the club's…"

"Don't worry about it, Jewel. You're part of the club. You're family. If you're in any danger, we take care of you. And that extends to your house guests."

She breathes out a sigh. "Thanks, Beast."

"Natalia," I say, leading her to the couch. "I have a question for you." I reach into my back pocket and pull out the small, shiny object I've brought with me. "Do you happen to recognize this?"

Reflexively, I start to look over to Olga for a translation, but before she can start, Natalia plucks the object out of my hand excitedly. She holds it up and exclaims something, then looks at me expectantly.

"She says it belongs to one of the other girls. Ashley," Olga tells me.

"Are you sure, Natalia?" I press her. "Are you totally sure it doesn't just look like the same ring?"

More talking between Olga and Natalia.

"*Nemaye*," Olga says, shaking her head. "Natalia say that Ashley loved this ring. She say it was her magic fortune ring."

Oh my God.

If Natalia is right, this is the first real evidence that the traffickers were operating out of the laundromat. And that both Natalia and the other girl — Ashley — were there.

"Thank you, Natalia," I say, squeezing her hand. "I have to take the ring back. But hopefully, we'll get to give it back to Ashley in person, very soon." I turn to Olga. "Thank you for translating. I'll try to be back soon."

While I've been talking to Natalia, Travis has gone into Jewel's kitchen. He's just getting off the phone when I come in.

"Angel's gonna send over Brick and Skid," he tells Jewel. "One guy stationed at each entrance. We'll keep a twenty-four seven watch until this is over." Turning to me, he continues. "You and me are gonna meet Angel in an hour."

I nod. "Drive me back to your place," I say. "I need my car."

25
BROOKE

My nerves are tingling as I ride behind Travis back to his place. It feels like a storm is about to break. Like I'm finally getting closer to some answers, after days of going nowhere.

Once I'm in my car, I follow Travis through Tanner Springs, past the road their clubhouse is on, and out of town. I had assumed we'd be going to the clubhouse, but I guess it makes sense that Angel might not want to talk to me there. We go about five miles out into the country, and Travis turns off onto a gravel road that leads to a small man-made lake where families like to take their kids on the weekends. The road makes a wide circle around the park where the lake is. We take it to the far end, where a lone motorcycle is parked not far from a picnic shelter.

Travis gets off his bike and I climb out of my car. A figure stands up from a picnic table. As we get closer, I recognize him as the man who thought I was Jewel's friend when I went to the clubhouse last time.

"Brother," Travis greets him. Angel nods but doesn't say anything.

"Mr…" I begin, holding out my hand.

"Angel." His voice is gruff. "Sit down."

I do as he says, watching as he straddles the table with one leg. He plants his boot on the bench in front of him.

"Talk," he grunts. "About why you came into my clubhouse pretendin' to be Jewel's friend."

I glance at Travis, but he doesn't say anything. It's clear he's gonna let the two of us tangle by ourselves.

"I assume Tr… *Beast*… has told you I'm in town investigating a sex trafficking ring. And that one of the girls who escaped the ring is currently at Jewel's apartment."

"Yeah."

This Angel guy is inscrutable as hell. I force myself not to be intimidated by him and continue.

"The thing is," I say, "this girl, um, *reacted* very strongly to the sight of Beast's cut when she was in the hospital. Through a translator — the girl doesn't speak very much English — she said it's the same cut that one of the men who was sexually abusing her — *raping* her — while she was being held captive wore."

He shakes his head, rolling his eyes. "There's plenty of clubs around here. The Lords aren't involved with shit like that."

"That's what Travis says," I nod. I glance at him, then back at Angel. "And I believe him, Angel. I'm *choosing* to take his word, and yours, that the *club* is not involved. For now." I draw myself up. "But that does not mean that no individual from your club is."

Angel's eyes grow cold. He tilts his head at me, appraisingly. "That's a hell of an accusation to make, without any proof."

"I don't have proof, you're right. But I do have a description, from the girl."

"You see anyone at the club that looked like that?"

"No. But I'm asking you. As vice-president. To tell me the truth. Is there anyone in your club who fits it?"

"What's this guy supposed to look like?" he smirks.

"Normal height. Older. Maybe fifties, or early sixties. A bit of a paunch. Black hair, with gray in it. Gray beard." I pause. "Tattoos. One of them the girl remembered more than the others. On his upper arm. A skull, with long hair and a bandana tied around his head. Pointing a gun."

The smirk is gone from Angel's face. His brow creases. One side of his jaw pulses.

He doesn't say anything for a second. Then another second. I glance over at Travis, to see he's staring at me in disbelief.

"Holy fuck," he rasps.

"What?" I ask, glancing back at Angel, who turns and nods grimly at Travis.

"Rock."

"Brooke, you gotta get out of here. Me and Angel need to talk." Travis has pulled me aside.

"Travis, I…"

"No arguments. Go." He frowns down at me.

"Goddamnit, Travis. Your VP just basically told me he knows who this man is!" I fling my hands out in frustration. "If you two want your club to be seen as innocent of being implicated in all this, you can't fucking protect this guy!"

"We're not protecting him!" he interrupts. "But we gotta figure out what to do here. This shit affects the club, too."

"Give me one good reason why I shouldn't just go haul this asshole into custody."

"Because we need time!"

"Time for what, goddamnit?"

"Time to figure out who the fuck these traffickers are!" He rakes a hand through his hair. "You think he's gonna tell you anything? Rock ain't gonna tell you jack shit! You haul him in today, you will not get one goddamn word outta him, no matter what you do. He's not fuckin' afraid of some feds. He's been in prison before. Shit, there ain't no way you can do anything to him that will break him!"

I take a step back, crossing my arms in front of me, and consider that he may be right. He obviously knows this Rock better than I do.

"You want information, B?" he growls. "You want to find out who these people are? Find the rest of these girls, and save them? Do you?"

"Yes," I shoot back.

"Then shut the hell up, go back to the hotel, and let me talk to Angel." His flashing eyes soften just a bit. "I'll come talk to you later. Okay?"

I heave a deep, defeated sigh. "Okay," I concede. "But I swear to God, do not leave me hanging, Travis."

"I'll be in touch as soon as I can."

"I give you until the end of the day."

I turn on my heel and walk back to the car. I'm still angry, but I'm trying to be hopeful that Travis will keep his word and get some answers for me.

I'm too antsy to go back to the hotel and just wait. So I decide to kill some time by taking the long way back.

I drive towards town slowly, for the first time really allowing myself to look around and reminisce about growing up here. It wasn't all bad. Not all the time. It's just that the things I have the strongest memories of are the ones I wish I could forget.

On an impulse, I turn the car at a crossroads and follow a narrow highway toward the north side of town. On the northeastern edge used to be the mobile home park I grew up in. I haven't been there in so long, I'm not even sure it's still there. But sure enough, pretty soon I see the faded wooden sign that announces the entrance to the place.

I drive in, slowing to look around. The park looks just different enough for me to know that I haven't gone back in time. Abstractly, I wonder how many of the people I knew back then still live here. I wonder how many of them would recognize me, or if I'd recognize them.

The trailer I lived in with my mom is still right where it was. It's been repainted, and it actually looks better than it did when we lived there. No one's outside, so I slow the car, pull it over to the side of the road, and stop. With the engine running, I look around at what used to be my world. The front steps where I used to sit and read are right there, just like they're waiting for me to come outside.

In my mind's eye, a boy on a dirt bike comes tearing around the bend in the road. The girl sitting on the steps looks up from her book, watching him as he hotdogs, popping wheelies and skidding around.

We were both so innocent then.

I wish more than anything that I could have stopped that little girl on the steps from having to suffer all the things she did. But I couldn't save her. All I could do was pick up the broken pieces as soon as she turned eighteen, and try to help her piece them back together.

Maybe in some ways, I'm still trying.

Maybe the reason I'm back here in the first place, trying to break this trafficking ring, isn't only to save some other broken girls. Maybe this whole thing has been about trying to save myself, too. Any one of those girls being held captive right now could have been me. A kid who fell through the cracks, and fell prey to some of the worst instincts of men.

I could have used someone to save me. To give me strength, and hope.

I think maybe I was looking to Travis to do that. But in the end, I never gave him a chance.

I stay there, lost in thought, until I see the curtains move in the living room window of the trailer next door. I realize I probably look pretty suspicious just sitting here. Putting my car into gear, I pull back out onto the road and finish my slow circuit around the mobile home park, feeling more wistful than I ever thought I would.

I'm almost back out on the main road when I notice there's a car behind me. It's a dark navy Dodge Charger, totally nondescript. My first thought is that it's an unmarked police car, and that someone in the park called in about a strange vehicle lurking around. I chuckle softly and wave my hand in the rearview mirror so he knows I'm not a threat, and then pull back out on the highway.

The car turns behind me, and starts to follow me at about five lengths behind. I shrug it off, figuring he'll tail me for a few blocks or so to make his point, and then turn back toward town. But that's not what happens. Frowning, I see he's pulling nearer, closing the distance to about three car lengths behind. Now I'm starting to get irritated. I prepare to see him whip out a dashboard flasher to pull me over. "Seriously, Rambo? Nothing better to do today?" I mutter.

But he doesn't do that either. At this point, I'm sick of it. I decide I'm going to keep driving out of town instead of turning back into Tanner Springs. He'll get tired of following me sooner or later, even if we have to cross the county line. I speed up a little — still respecting the limit — and come to the crest of a hill that marks the unofficial northern city limits.

Once we're over the hill, the car tailing me speeds up, rapidly.

My stomach twists in alarm.

Suddenly I realize this isn't just a self-important cop trying to teach me a lesson.

And I've just driven away from town and isolated myself.

I check the road in front of me; there's no other vehicles visible on either side. Gripping the wheel, I punch on the accelerator. I feel the engine goose ahead as I put a quick ten miles on my speed. The car behind me falls back. Then, a second or two later, it starts to speed up again. *Fuck*. I opted to take my own car down here instead of a fleet vehicle, and my engine is no match for the Charger's. I push the accelerator to the floor, to put as much distance between us as possible. But the Charger catches up easily. It pulls into the left lane, and starts to gain on me. Thinking quickly, I wrench the wheel to the left, straddling the center line so he can't pass me. He swerves and falls back, then starts to gain again.

A solid thump to the back of my car jars my neck. I cry out and grab the wheel tighter so I don't lose control. The Charger falls back, then speeds up and hits me again, harder this time. I swerve, the back of my car fishtailing a little. He's going to damage the chassis soon, and if he does I won't be able to keep the car on the road. This isn't sustainable. I'm going too fast to turn, and I can't outrun him. I have to figure out another plan.

In desperation, I scan the road ahead for a place to pull off, but there's nothing. At the top of the next hill, the Charger hits me a third time, and the impact makes one of my rear tires blow. *This is it.*

Then I'm skidding, the car veering onto the gravel shoulder on its own. I brace myself for impact as the front wheels fly over the side, into the air. My stomach drops as the car starts to fall, and as I go over the edge and the unknown, a raw cry rips from my throat:

"*Travis!*"

26
BEAST

I watch Brooke as she gets in her car and leaves. When she's gone, Angel comes up behind me.

Silently, we mount our bikes and head to the clubhouse.

There ain't nothing to say right now. Not until we get some answers.

That doesn't mean that I'm not ready to explode. To purge the shit that's coursing through my veins like poison.

Anger. Disbelief. Disgust.

I can't believe Rock was raping little girls. But there's no other way to explain what Brooke just told us.

I have no fucking idea what's going on. And I'm pretty sure I don't want to.

But whatever it is, we have to get to the bottom of it. For the good of those little girls, and for the club.

Angel and I head straight up the stairs as soon as we get to the clubhouse. As we climb, I hear Rock's voice shouting through the closed door of his apartment.

"You knew!" he's roaring. "I don't fuckin' care! You knew they were gunning for the Lords! You got me into this, you fuckin' piece of shit! You set me up! You set my fuckin' club up!"

Angel frowns at me. Inside, no voice answers Rock, so he must be on the phone.

"You listen to me, you asshole," Rock continues. "You think you got the upper hand now, but I will fuckin' *end* you, you hear me? I will end you!"

There's a loud crash, followed by a string of obscenities. Angel waits a couple seconds, then pounds on the door.

"Rock! You in there? I need to talk to you."

Rock comes to the door. "Yeah?" he growls. He's face is red, and contorted into a scowl. He's wearing a black Harley T-shirt and faded jeans. Just below the left sleeve, the bottom half of the tattoo Natalia saw is visible. My stomach wrenches in disgust.

"Can we come in?"

Rock glances from Angel to me. "Sure," he says, stepping back so we can enter. "What's up?"

Angel pauses. "You sounded pretty mad just now. Something wrong?"

"Nah, nah. Everything's good."

"Yeah? Who were you talking to?"

Rock bristles. "Ain't none of your business."

"No?" Angel challenges. I can see him starting to get angry. "You were talkin' about the club, brother. About us bein' set up. I think that means it *is* our business."

"Listen, you asshole, I'm the president of this club," Rock spits out, jabbing his own chest with his thumb. "You fuckin' answer to *me*, you got that? Not the other way around."

"Yeah," Angel nods, with a slight sneer. "I got that." He takes a step forward. "Okay, Rock. Let's change the subject. Talk about what we came to talk to you about."

Rock relaxes a little. "Okay. What do you need?"

Angel walks over to the small living room and takes a seat in one of the chairs. He motions for us to follow. I take the other chair, and Rock settles down on the couch.

"So, we got a little problem. The *club* does." Angel leans forward, elbows on knees, steepling his fingers. "I don't know if you heard about this when you were in the hospital, but there's an FBI agent in town. She's been investigating a trafficking ring." He pauses. "A sex trafficking ring."

Rock's face goes stony. "Yeah?"

"Yeah." Angel looks at Rock for a long moment. "See, the thing is, one of the girls who was being kept in this ring, she escaped. And she's been talking to this fed chick. Apparently, she was able to describe one of the men who was fuckin' her in this ring." He leans back in his seat, and fists one hand in the other, cracking his knuckles. "Lords of Carnage cut. Gray hair. White beard. Tattoo of a skull pointin' a gun on his left arm." He pauses. "Kind of specific, don't you think?"

Rock snorts. "Yeah. That's pretty specific. So?"

I cock my head, barely believing what I just heard. "So? You don't think this is a problem?"

He shrugs. "Lots of guys in MCs around here. Lots of guys with tats." He smirks. "And ink can be changed."

"Jesus fuck, Rock," Angel mutters in disgust. "These chicks are just kids, most of them. What the fuck is wrong with you?"

"They were old enough!" Rock shoots back. "And since when did you turn into the goddamn Virgin Mary?"

"I ain't no Virgin Mary, Rock, but at least I've got some goddamn limits! You know how old this kid was? Sixteen!"

He's out of his seat now, shouting. "Fuckin' sixteen! You piece of shit!"

I stand up and put a hand on Angel's shoulder. I'm practically shaking with anger, but I know we have to find out what Rock knows about this trafficking ring. We need to find out who else is involved.

"Angel, brother." He shoots me a look of barely concealed rage, but stops shouting. I sit back down as he starts pacing the room. "Rock," I say, working to control myself. "Who the fuck are these guys? Who's trafficking these girls?"

"That ain't important," Rock shrugs. "The club ain't involved, right? This is my business."

"NO."

Rock and I turn to Angel. His face is furious.

And he's got Rock's cell phone in his hand.

"The club's involved, Rock. And you're gonna tell us what's going on."

"Fuck you, Angel," Rock says, rising. "You give me that goddamn…"

But before he can finish his sentence, Rock freezes in his tracks.

In Angel's other hand is his piece. And he's pointing it at our president.

"Beast," he says, holding Rock's cell out to me. "Dial the last number Rock was talking to. Put it on speaker."

"NO!" Rock shouts, but Angel cocks the gun and holds it higher, aiming it at Rock's head.

"Do it, Beast," he says.

I look from one man to the other.

One of these men is a traitor to the club. Whoever it is will be cast out in disgrace. Or worse.

And depending on my choice, so will I.

Reaching toward Angel, I take the phone from him.

I hit the last number Rock called and put it on speaker. The phone rings once, then picks up. An angry voice answers.

"What the fuck, Rock? We're done here. I told you that."

Jesus Christ.

I end the call and look at Angel. His lip curls as he stares at Rock.

"Holloway," he laughs coldly, shaking his head in disbelief. "Jarred fuckin' Holloway."

"I will kill you right fucking now, Rock." Angel stands above him, like the avenging angel he's named after. "Unless you talk. That's your only chance of getting out of this room alive."

"This ain't what you think!" Rock insists. "I'll tell you everything, but this was all about keepin' the club safe!"

"Then you got nothing to worry about by telling us." Angel leans against the wall. "Go. Before I get sick of holdin' this gun and decide to do something about it."

"The ring is Dragon's."

"The Outlaw Sons?"

"Yeah." He nods. "And Holloway's involved, too."

"What the fuck?"

"Holloway gave them a place to operate out of in Tanner Springs." Rock's eyes move back and forth between us. "A laundromat that was a good front because no one ever went there. Holloway came to me and told me he wanted to broker a deal between our two clubs. Get us cooperatin'. The deal was, Holloway would stop ridin' the Lords' asses and look the other way, and in exchange he'd get a small cut of our profits. And, a larger percentage of the cut from the sex ring."

"Jesus Christ…" I breathe. "You fuckin' cut a deal with the mayor, without tellin' us."

"It was just an agreement! He looks the other way and we're all good! But that fucker sold us out," Rock seethes. "He was workin' with the Outlaw Sons the whole time. To end the Lords, and let the Sons move into our territory once we're wiped out." His eyes are like dark stones. "I want that fucker destroyed. Holloway is a fuckin' dead man."

"You fuckin' cut a deal with the mayor. Without the club." Angel is shaking his head. His tone is flat, emotionless. "Did you actually think you could get Holloway under your thumb, the way you had my dad when he was mayor?"

"I thought I could strike a deal," Rock retorts. "The club wasn't too sure about your dad back in the day, either!"

"But at least you fuckin' *told* the club you were dealing with Abe!" Angel bites out. "You did all this behind the club's back!"

"I did it for the Lords…"

"You *betrayed* the Lords!"

The look of hatred on Angel's face is so complete, for a second I think he's gonna shoot Rock. His pistol is aimed directly at our president's head. Rock freezes, staring down the barrel of the gun.

"Holloway sold you down the river," Angel rasps. "Sold us into a war. And you walked us right into it."

In my pocket, my phone buzzes. I ignore it.

"I should fuckin' kill you right now," Angel tells Rock. "But I'm not going to. The club will decide your fate."

Rock pales. "The Lords will know I did this for them," he says, but his tone says he knows otherwise.

"We'll see." Angel nods at me. "Beast. Go call up a couple of the men to stand guard outside Rock's door until I can call church."

I walk out of Rock's apartment, knowing that as soon as I do this, the Lords of Carnage will never be the same.

Downstairs, I find Tank and Striker.

"Brothers, something's up," I say. "Angel sent me down here to get two men to stand guard outside Rock's door." I pause. "Make sure he doesn't try to leave."

The two men stare at me. "Are you fucking serious?" Tank murmurs.

"Yeah." I take a deep breath. "I know what I'm asking you. I know it ain't an easy thing for you to say yes to. But some serious shit has gone down. We need to call church."

"Fuck." Striker reaches up and rubs his neck. "Fuck. Yeah. Okay."

I look at Tank.

He pauses a beat, then nods, looking somber. "Yeah."

The three of us head upstairs. Tank and Striker stay outside, while I go in. Angel's still got his gun trained on Rock. I frisk him, finding a knife in his boot, and grab the gun that's sitting on the table in the kitchenette.

"You brought the FBI down on us, too, Rock," Angel's saying as we get up to leave. "You're gonna have to answer for that in church, too."

I don't know what I expect Rock's reaction to be, but he actually *laughs.*

"That's the least of our problems," he says. "If we go down, Holloway goes down, and he knows it. His men are takin' care of the FBI gash."

I freeze. "What?" I snarl.

"She ain't gonna be able to tell anybody jack shit," Rock continues with a shrug. "If she's still alive, she ain't gonna be for long."

"Motherfucker!" I shout. I take a step toward him. Suddenly, I don't care about doing the right thing. I don't care about club justice. I just want to wrap my hands around his throat and watch the life go out of his eyes.

"Beast!"

Someone is pounding at the door. Jewel's muffled voice is calling my name. Giving Rock a murderous look, I turn and grab the knob, flinging it open.

"They said you were up here! Oh, thank God!" Jewel's eyes are wide, her face pale. "You have to go! It's Brooke! Her car's been run off the road!"

27
BROOKE

The pain in my chest is intense, almost blinding. The air bag that's deployed from my steering wheel has knocked all the wind out of me. I can hardly breathe, and an acrid stench pollutes the small amount of air I can get into my lungs.

I groan against the throb, forcing my eyes open. The car's listing at an angle, my right side about forty-five degrees lower than my left. I'm in a deep ditch, next to what I think is a field, though all I can see through the passenger window is dirt and grass.

I turn my head to look around. A slice of pain lances through my ribs, making me gasp. I can't tell much about my lower body, trapped as it is by the car. I force myself not to let my mind go down that path.

Through the fog of my agony, it's an effort to think clearly, but a spike of fear reaches my brain as I remember the car that ran me off the road and realize what's coming for me.

Wincing but determined, I contort my body enough to lift my right arm up toward my waist. I peer through the windows of the driver's side, just in time to see the figure come over the ridge of earth at the top of the ditch. His face is twisted into a determined mask of anger. I know he's come to kill me. I know I won't make it out of here alive.

A strangled scream forces itself through my lips as I struggle against the air bag and belt. Desperately, I claw against the fabric of the bag, pushing my hand between it and my stomach. He comes closer, sidestepping his way down the embankment toward the car. He's large, and strong-looking, and I know in my injured state I won't stand a chance fighting him if it comes to that.

He reaches the bottom. When he peers through the windshield, his eyes lock on mine. The terror on my face must show, because he grins — a leer of triumph. Of *pleasure* — in anticipation of the pain he's about to inflict.

My stomach roils. I inch my hand forward, my eyes not leaving his face.

Just as he reaches for the handle of my door, my gaze slips downward, just a couple of inches. What I see makes an electric jolt run through me.

Scratch marks, on his cheek.

This isn't the first time we've met, he and I.

But it will be the last.

The handle of the door clicks, just as my fingers close around their target. The man's eyes drop for a second as he realizes the door is locked, but then he looks at me again, grinning monstrously. *The lock can't protect you.* He reaches behind himself, toward his back waistband, and as he does I drag my hand upward, say a prayer, and fire.

A deafening roar blocks out everything for a few seconds. Glass shatters all around me. I scream, but it makes no sound.

Then the glass stops falling. I realize my eyes are squeezed shut. I take a juddering breath and open them.

The airbag has deflated, and drapes limply over me like a thin blanket. The driver's side window is completely shot out.

Through the angle of the opening, I can only see the top of the man's head. He's lying on the ground. He's not moving. A few feet away, I see some red spatters of what must be blood.

The only sound I can hear is a distant ringing. I try to take another breath, but even without the airbag trapping me, I still can't get a full lungful of air without the pain slicing through me.

I start to cry. The sound coming from inside me seems to be miles away. It scares me, so I make myself stop.

I'm starting to get dizzy. I don't know if it's lack of air, or adrenaline, or something else I am too afraid to contemplate.

Phone, I mouth.

It takes me a couple of minutes to dig it out of my pocket. The whole time I'm getting dizzier, the pain so bad I'm afraid I'll pass out. Finally I manage to pull it up to my face. I can barely think. I want Travis, but I don't have his number. So I try the next best thing.

Fumbling a bit, I push on her name on the screen. I still can't hear, so I stare at the words until they say the call has started.

"Jewel," I croak into the speaker. "I need Travis. I've been in a car accident. I'm on old Highway Fourteen, about… three miles north of town, I think." I start to cry again. "Please, please, send him. I need… help… I think…"

Then suddenly it feels like I'm falling, and I drop the phone. Blackness overtakes me, and I drift into nothingness.

* * *

I'm awakened by a searing pain, like I'm being stabbed. I cry out, and try to fight my assailant, but a deep familiar voice stops me.

"Babe, stay with me," he croons. "I've got you. I've got you, B."

I realize I'm being carried. His warm, strong arms hold me against his chest.

"Travis," I gasp, tears pricking my eyes. "I…"

"Sshhh," he stops me, murmuring against my ear. "Save your strength. We'll talk later. You're safe. Just relax."

"It hurts so bad…"

"I know. The pain will stop soon. I promise."

I sink against him, praying that he's telling me the truth, and let the darkness take me again.

* * *

When I wake up again, I feel like I'm sinking in dark water. Everything's blurry. It's impossible to move my limbs. The pain is still there, but it's far away.

"Is she coming around?" a female voice says.

"Babe?"

"Travis…" I whisper.

"How you feelin'?"

I swallow painfully. "Like death."

He chuckles. "You came pretty close back there. But you'll live."

"Unfortunately," I joke. With an effort, I open my eyes. He's blurry, but it's definitely him. There's a figure next to him, too.

"Jewel?" I ask, just to be sure.

"Hey, there! You had us scared for a while." She reaches down and squeezes my hand. "You're a badass, you know that?"

I try a laugh, but it hurts so bad I end up gasping. "I don't feel very badass right now."

"Well, you are." Jewel looks down at me and gives me a teary smile. "Natalia and Olga are going to be really relieved you're okay." She glances over at Travis. "I'm gonna leave you two alone, now that I've seen for myself that Brooke is awake." She gives my hand one more squeeze and lets go. "You get some rest now, okay?"

I nod. "Jewel?"

"Yes?"

"Thank you," I take a shallow breath. "I might not be here if you hadn't answered your phone."

"Don't say that, honey," she whispered. "But I'm glad I did."

Jewel quietly slips out of the room, closing the door behind her. Beast and I watch her go, and then he turns to me.

"Seems like we've been spending a hell of a lot of time in this hospital," he remarks, one corner of his mouth turning up.

"Yeah. I have to say, I'm not a fan." I try to adjust myself in the bed, then grimace. "So, I'm guessing I broke a rib or two?"

"Four," he corrects. "And fractured your sternum."

"Shit," I hiss. "No wonder it hurts so bad."

"Yeah. You're on a lot of pain meds, though. So it should keep the worst of it away."

Now that we're alone, my mind races back to the accident. "Travis," I say suddenly, "what happened to the man who was after me?"

"You got him." His face clouds over. "That son of a bitch will never hurt anyone again."

"He had scratch marks on his cheek! He was the one who came after me in my hotel room."

Travis nods. "Not surprised. Though, what was a surprise was who he is. *Was*," he corrects himself.

"Who?"

"Officer Rob Johannsen." Travis shakes his head. "Of the Tanner Springs Police Department, and underling to Chief Brandt Crup."

"What?"

I sit bolt upright in the bed. The knife of pain is immediate, making me gasp and clutch at the mattress. "Holy shit," I wheeze as I wait for it to pass.

"Jesus, Brooke." Travis is up and helping me lie back down in an instant. "You gotta be more careful." I collapse back against the mattress and close my eyes for a few seconds, trying to breathe through it. Eventually the pain starts to subside, and I open my eyes again.

"Travis, you have to tell me what's going on," I pant. "How could a cop be involved in this?"

"A lot went down today, babe," he murmurs. "Turns out, there was way more going on behind the scenes than anyone knew. But you should rest," he says, shaking his head. "I can tell you later."

"Travis Carr, I swear to God, if you don't tell me, I'll get up out of this bed and find out myself!" I insist. "I won't be able to rest until I know what's going on, and you know it. So if you want me to have any hope of it, you better start talking."

"There's a hell of a lot," he frowns. "But I'll tell you what I know so far."

I lean back against the pillows and sigh. "Okay. Good. So, go."

His jaw tenses for a second. "Well. First of all. The guy Natalia said was rapin' her. With the club cut." He pauses, and his eyes grow dark and angry. "We confirmed who it was."

"Who?"

His eyes lock on mine. "Our club president."

"*What?!*"

"Yeah." Travis's face grows dark, murderous. "None of us knew. When you told us how Natalia described him, Angel and I realized right away it was him." His lip curls in disgust. "We went to talk to him, back at our clubhouse, and we caught him in the middle of a phone conversation where he was sayin' some pretty fucked up things. Come to find out, he was talkin' to the mayor. Jarred Holloway." Travis waits a beat, then leans in and looks at me. "Holloway is one of the kingpins of this trafficking ring, Brooke. And the cops are involved. Or at least, Chief Crup is. That's why Johannsen ran you off the road. They were gonna kill you because you were getting too close."

I gape at him. "Oh my God. The mayor, *and* the police, *and* your club president? How is that possible?"

He snorts, and shakes his head. "That ain't all. But that's the part I can tell you."

"Travis, we have to break this ring open!" I cry. "We have to do something, now!"

"Already being handled, Brooke."

"How?"

He pauses, weighing his words. "Look. There's parts of this you can't know. Club business, that I can't tell you. But what I can tell you is, the Lords are gonna deliver the ring to the authorities. The people involved are gonna get served justice." His jaw sets. "And those girls are gonna get free. *All* of them."

"But…"

"Sshhh…" he interrupts me. "Brooke. You've gotta get some rest. I can't tell you more right now. But I promise you. It's being handled. And I'll tell you what I can, as soon as I can." He takes my hand in his large one. "Do you trust me?" he asks.

I close my eyes for a few moments. When I open them, his rough, handsome face is all I can see.

"Yes," I breathe. "I trust you."

"Good." He leans over and kisses me. It's soft and gentle, unlike any kiss he's ever given me before. From far away, through the haze of drugs, a ribbon of desire threads its way through me. "It's all gonna be good, Brooke." He leans back. "Now, rest."

"Okay," I say softly. I don't want to sleep, but I really am exhausted. "Will I see you later, then?"

"Me?" he asks in surprise. "I ain't leavin' your side." He chuckles. "Now shut up and sleep, Brooke. Get better for me. I need you healthy again."

Obediently, I close my eyes, feeling safe and happy that he's going to stay here with me. As I drift off, I replay his words in my head. Or at least the ones I most want to hear.

"Get better for me. I need you healthy again."

"Get better for me. I need you…"

"I need you…"

28
BEAST

Angel calls the Lords to church without me, because I'm not about to leave Brooke's fucking side right now. When visiting hours end, I tell the nurses who try to get me to leave that I'm not budging, and they can bring every goddamn security guard in the hospital in but it won't change anything. Eventually, I think Isabel pulls the other nurses aside and talks them into leaving us the hell alone.

I spend the night in a goddamn uncomfortable chair, but I don't give a shit. I know Brooke's gonna be okay. Her injuries aren't life-threatening, and they'll heal. But I can't get it out of my mind how close I came to losing her. If she hadn't managed to shoot Rob Johannsen, he would have killed her for sure.

I stay there with her all night, and through the next day. Whenever a nurse or a doc comes in, I go grab some shitty food from the cafeteria and then come back. I want my face to be the first thing she sees whenever she wakes up.

Sometime the next afternoon, while Brooke's napping, there's a soft rap on the door. I look up to see Angel stick his head through. He lifts his chin in greeting. I push myself out of the chair and go outside to talk to him.

"How's she doin'?" he asks me.

"On the mend. She's tough; she'll be okay."

"Glad to hear it."

Angel's face is stony. This ain't a social call, and we both know it. Better to get it over with.

"So," I mutter. "Church yesterday."

"Yeah." He reaches up and rubs the back of his neck. "Listen, let's go outside and talk about this." He looks around. "Better not to have any ears around us."

I want to refuse, but I know he's right. We stop off at the nurses' station on the way out and I tell Isabel we're goin' out for a smoke. Angel and I head outside and go find a bench about a hundred feet from the front entrance, where there's no one else nearby to hear us.

"Rock pleaded his case to the Lords," Angel says, lighting up. "He told them everything he told us. He tried to stretch the truth a few times, but I made sure he did right by the brothers."

"And?"

"They voted to remove him as president. Unanimous." He takes a deep drag and blows it out. "And they voted club justice."

I knew this was coming. There wasn't any other way it could have gone. Rock gets the death penalty for betraying the Lords.

"When?" I ask tiredly.

"Today."

I think about what Angel said a few days ago, about Rock being like a father to him. Hell, as president, he was a father to us all. A tough one, and sometimes a questionable one. But still, a father.

Now, he has to pay the ultimate price, for breaking faith with his family. A bullet to the head.

"Shit." I shake my head.

"Yeah." Angel sounds grim. He laughs, but there's no humor in it. "My first act as president."

Goddamn. What a hell of a way to start.

"You want me to be there?" I ask. "I can get away for a couple hours."

"Nah." Angel shrugs. "That ain't why I'm here. I wanted to give you this." He reaches into his pocket and pulls out an envelope.

"What is it?" I ask as he hands it to me.

"It's all the info Brooke needs to take down the trafficking ring." Angel looks out at the parking lot. "Names, details, locations. Enough to put Holloway away. And Crup. And every other corrupt son of a bitch involved. Rock gave it all up." He blows out a breath. "Not without a little convincing."

"Thanks. I'll make sure she knows this is in exchange for keeping the club out of it."

"Good."

I stare at the clean white paper, thinking about everything that's so dirty inside of it. The filth that lives inside of men. Especially the ones who look the purest on the outside, sometimes.

"I had a question to ask you, too, Beast. A favor."

"What is it?"

Angel tosses his cigarette on the ground and turns to me. "I want you to be my VP."

I stare at him, not comprehending for a second. "Me?" I finally ask, shaking my head once in confusion. "I would have thought you'd choose Ghost." Ghost, after all, has been Rock's Sergeant at Arms for years. And he's been Angel's best friend for even longer.

"I need Ghost as my Sergeant," Angel says. "There ain't no one better for that job. Rock picked well on that one." He gives a soft snort. "But what I need in a vice-president is someone who ain't afraid to challenge me. Who's gonna tell me the truth, no matter what. And who I can trust, one-hundred percent." He lifts his chin. "That's you, brother."

"Shit, Angel. I don't know what to say. I'm fuckin' honored." And I am. I know what a responsibility the job of vice-president is. If Angel thinks I can do a good job of it, I'll bust my ass to prove him right. "There's just one problem, though," I continue, knowing I have to say it. "And she's sleepin' upstairs in that hospital room."

"Yeah," Angel nods. "We gotta talk about that. What's happenin' between the two of you anyway?"

"Not sure," I say.

But that ain't quite true.

I *do* know.

I'm in love with her. But that's nothing new. I always fucking have been. As much as I've tried to tell myself the opposite, I know that now.

But loving her didn't stop her from leaving me all those years ago.

It doesn't change the fact that she's a fucking federal agent. And I'm an outlaw.

It doesn't change the fact that I can't compromise my MC. As long as Brooke is FBI, I'll have to choose one or the other.

"Angel," I begin, but then stop. I don't want to let him down, but I can't say yes or no right now. Finally, I say what I need. "Will you let me think about it for a couple days?"

He seems to understand what I'm asking.

"I'd hate to lose you, Beast. The club needs you now."

"The club needs a VP who's all in," I answer gravely. "After this shit with Rock, the Lords need that more than ever. I ain't gonna accept a job I can't do the way it needs to be done." I pause. "I just need to make sure I can do that."

Angel nods. "I respect that, brother."

"Thanks."

We sit for a moment, not speaking. Finally, he puts his hands on his knees and stands. "Well. I'm gonna take off. I, ah, got some shit I gotta do."

I stand and face him. "I don't envy you, Angel." I hold out my hand and he takes it. Somberly, we shake.

"I'll let you know my decision soon," I tell him.

"All right." His eyes meet mine. "I'll let you know when it's done."

And so, Angel walks off, to do the hardest thing a president ever has to do for his club.

And I go back upstairs, to wait for Brooke to wake up.

* * *

When I get back to her room, there's a doctor in there with her. He glances over at me as I come in, his eyes sliding down to rest on my cut. I'm about to give him some attitude when Brooke calls my name.

"The doctor says I can probably get out of the hospital today!" she tells me.

I'm surprised. "That right?" I ask.

The doc glances toward her, and then back at me. "Are you a friend of Ms. Brentano's?"

"Yes," I bark. I'm not in the mood for any bullshit.

"Well," he continues in a professional voice, turning back to Brooke. "We've determined there's no trauma to the lungs, which was what we were most concerned about. There's bruising, of course, and you'll be in some pain for two to three weeks, though of course we'll give you a prescription for that. Within about six weeks, you'll be feeling close to normal again, provided you're careful and don't overdo it."

He tells us he'll go process her paperwork to be discharged, and asks if she has someone to drive her home.

Brooke looks at me, a little sheepishly, with a question in her eyes.

"That depends," I say gruffly. "You think you can hang onto the back of my bike?"

The doc looks at me, alarmed. Brooke bursts out laughing, then lets out a yelp of pain. "Dammit, Travis, don't *do* that!" she complains.

"Sorry, couldn't resist," I chuckle. "I am gonna have to go get a car, though. Can you sit tight until then?"

"I'm not going anywhere," she says wryly.

The doc leaves, looking a little unsettled. Once he's out the door, I snort and shake my head. "Damn, I really think he believed I was just gonna strap you onto the back of my Harley."

"He definitely looked a little nervous around you," Brooke agrees, clearly amused. "But seriously, don't make me laugh anymore, okay? It really hurts."

"Sorry, babe." I say, and sit down on the bed.

"So," she says in a small voice. "Are you gonna take me back to the hotel?"

"Nah," I reply. "I figured you could stay a while at my place. You know, as long as you don't take up a lot of space."

"It'd be just for a couple of days," she promises. "Until I heal up enough to be able to drive a car."

"You know your car is toast, right?"

"Yeah, I know." She shrugs. "I meant, until I can rent one."

"Tell you what," I suggest. "Let's talk about that when we're back at my place. I got some other stuff I wanted to tell you about."

She nods. "Me, too," she says softly. "That would be good."

I ride over to Twisted Pipes and pick up a vehicle to bring Brooke home in. I choose a low, comfortable Lincoln Town Car that should be pretty easy for her to get into and out of. When I come back, she's already been discharged. I help her into a wheelchair, carefully load her into the front seat, and take her to my place.

When we pull up to the house, I realize she's gonna have a tough time climbing the stairs to the second floor. But she's a trouper and makes it all the way by herself, with me following behind her just in case. I get her set up on the couch, then sit down beside her.

I don't give her the envelope yet. I tell Brooke everything else I can about who's in charge of the trafficking ring. And that Angel has enough info for her that she can take the whole thing down. All of it, delivered on a silver platter that she can hand to her boss.

"But it's with the understanding that the Lords of Carnage is left completely out of it, Brooke. Because it was only Rock who was involved." I pause. "And he's being dealt with."

"What does that mean?"

"It means it's our business. And if you pull the law into our business, people are just gonna get hurt. It won't help anything, Brooke. It'll just muddy the waters."

"I *am* the law, Travis." Her eyes grow dark. "Or at least, I was. I'm not sure what I am anymore. I just… I just want justice for these girls. For Natalia."

"The law ain't the same as justice, babe." I reach up and push away a lock of hair that's fallen into her face. "Sometimes you can get justice through the law. But more often than not, the law's just an excuse for the people who are already in power to stay in power. It's a set of rules for them to hide behind. To use for their own advantage." I brush my thumb against her jawline. "Justice is different. Justice doesn't let the predators hide behind the prey." I shake my head. "Rock's gonna get justice. Club justice. Holloway and those other motherfuckers, you can have. Bring them to justice. If you're able to."

Brooke is silent, absorbing my words. We sit like that for a few minutes without talking. Eventually she leans toward me and lays her head on my shoulder. I take her in my arms, being careful not to hurt her.

"I'm not sure I can do this anymore," she says in a small, quiet voice.

I've been waiting for it since the first day we had sex. But when she says it, the words still hit me like a freight train.

"Okay," I say. Keeping my voice neutral is killing me, but I do it. "You can sleep in the bed for the night. I'll take the couch."

"No. I mean I'm not sure I can work for the bureau anymore."

"Are you serious?" I ask. "You're thinking about quitting?"

Wordlessly, she nods against my shoulder.

I almost laugh, I'm so fuckin' relieved.

"Okay. So, what will you do?"

"I don't know." I feel her shrug, then wince a little. "But… I was thinking maybe I'd stick around in Tanner Springs awhile while I think about it."

"Yeah?" My voice turns hoarse. "You need a place to stay?"

"The Courtyard Inn is getting a little old," she admits. "And I'm sick of eating in restaurants."

"Maybe we could make an arrangement," I suggest. "I could let you stay here for a while." I wait a beat. "In exchange for paying me rent, of course."

She starts to giggle, and then the pain makes her stop and she bitches me out for making her laugh.

And I feel better than I've felt since the day I met Brooke Fucking Brentano.

29
BROOKE

In the days after I move in with Travis, I think a lot about what he said regarding justice, and what it means. I decide he's right. It's not the same thing as law.

If I turned in Rock's name with all the rest, the law would catch the club in its net.

Justice, on the other hand, would recognize that it was the Lords who helped bring down the trafficking ring in the first place.

I joined the FBI because I wanted justice for victims. Because I was one myself once, but I never got it.

Now I realize this isn't what I want to do anymore. I don't want to be a cog in a legal machine.

I want something more.

What that is, I'm not quite sure.

But I think maybe coming back to the town I fled — to face my demons — is the first step.

To face my demons, and to correct the biggest mistake I ever made.

For a few days, Travis takes care of me, even though I insist I'm able to manage by myself. He gives me the envelope with the names of the traffickers, and I call Lafontaine and feed it all to him, with enough detail that he has no choice but to send a team down to break open the case and arrest all those involved.

Mayor Jarred Holloway was one of the first to be arrested. When they seized his computer as part of the investigation, they ended up finding a cache of child pornography. Some of the videos and images were of kids who weren't even in puberty yet. His wife, Annelise Holloway, was apparently traumatized by the whole affair. She immediately filed for divorce and full custody of their two daughters on the basis of the child porn in his possession.

As I promised Travis, I left Rock Anthony's name out of the information I gave Lafontaine. I let the Lords of Carnage mete out their own justice, which in the end equaled death. Rock was found in a hotel room a couple of towns over, dead from a bullet to the head. The death was officially ruled a suicide. No further investigation was done.

Natalia's father arrived from Ukraine to take her home. She was reunited with a few of the other girls from the trafficking ring, including another girl from Kiev, Katya. They gave full testimonies, before being sent back home on the FBI's dime. I got to meet Katya, as well as most of the other girls who had been held captive. I even got to give Ashley her sparkly ring back. That girl was, and is, tough as nails. She was a witness at the trial, and gave a testimony so damning that it helped put the traffickers away for a good long time.

One of the other girls who was found as a result of breaking the case was the cousin of a woman who works at one of the local tattoo places in town. The girl, Zoe, wasn't being held with the rest of them, but she was being prostituted by a man associated with the ring, in a shady area of Cleveland. She's back at home now. Doing okay, I guess. Though it's hard to imagine how she's gonna go back to being just a little girl now. That's true for all of them.

I hope they manage it.

A full-scale investigation into the Tanner Springs Police Department followed from the revelations that Chief Crup and Robert Johannsen were involved in the cover-up. Since Johannsen attempted to murder me to shut me up, and I ended up shooting him in self-defense, I was taken off the case almost immediately. I resigned from the agency shortly thereafter. Lafontaine didn't try to stop me, and I didn't expect him to.

There were some rumors going around in Tanner Springs about me being asked to join the police force afterwards. To help clean things up, and make sure the corruption was a thing of the past. The truth is, yes, I was asked. I turned them down. I don't know exactly what my future plans are, but I think it's safe to say that my law enforcement career is over.

Travis, at Angel's request, accepted the position as VP of the club. When it came out that he and I were involved, and that I was FBI — *ex*-FBI — there was a little grumbling, which I expected. What I *didn't* expect was that Angel quashed it immediately, saying that anyone who had a problem with me had a problem with him.

Isabel even brought me into the fold with the women of the club. Even though I wasn't technically an old lady, they welcomed me with open arms — going so far as giving me shit about Beast and asking what it was like in bed with a monster like him.

I didn't kiss and tell.

Not *too* much, anyway.

And when, a few weeks later, Gunner's old lady Alix went into labor, I was right there at the hospital with everyone else.

It's a girl, by the way. Her name is Olivia.

* * *

The day after the birth, Travis and I go back to the hospital to see the new family. Walking down the now-familiar halls, my mind keeps flashing to all the times I've been here since I got back to Tanner Springs. This is the first time that the reason we're here is a good one. One full of hope for the future, unmarred by the pain of the past.

As we chat with a tired but radiant Alix, I look over at Gunner holding little Olivia. The baby seems impossibly small in his huge, muscled arms. I can't help but glance at Travis — who's the biggest member of the Lords by far — and wonder what it would look like to see him cradling an infant. Just at that moment, Travis glances over, and his eyes meet mine. I look away, not wanting him to read my thoughts. I feel heat rise to my cheeks as I listen to Alix tell me they've decided that Olivia's middle name will be Lucy, after Gunner's mom.

We don't stay at the hospital too long. We know we're only a couple people in a long line of well-wishers the three of them will have that day. So we say our goodbyes and tell them we'll see them later. Then we leave them to prepare for the next visit.

On the way out, we pass by the hospital pharmacy. "You need any more pain pills, since we're here?" Travis asks me.

"No," I answer. "I still have a few left. And I think I'm healed enough to stop taking them, anyway. I can get by on Ibuprofen from here on out."

We haven't really talked about what would happen once I recovered from my injuries, Travis and I. Mostly, we've just continued on like our living situation was totally normal. He and I have been sleeping in the same bed since that first night. At first, I was in too much agony to do anything except try to find a comfortable position so I wouldn't lie awake all night. But once the pain began to subside a little, having him so near me without touching me started to feel a little like torture. I knew he was feeling the same way because I saw the evidence through the tight boxer-briefs he wore to bed. But I also knew he wasn't going to touch me until he was sure he wouldn't hurt me. Eventually, neither one of us could take it anymore. We've been having careful but still explosive sex since then — *much* more often than my doctor would probably advise.

"Gun looks happy as hell," Travis murmurs as he opens the passenger-side door of the car for me to climb inside. "Never would have imagined him as a dad before he met Alix."

"They're a great fit for each other," I agree. "You know, I would have thought he'd be all about having a boy, but he looks pretty enamored with little Olivia."

Travis walks to the other side and gets in. He starts the car and puts it in gear. "You ever think about kids?" he asks nonchalantly.

"Not really," I say. And it's true. But right now, with him asking it, my heart constricts a little at the idea of me being a family with Travis and a little one. Just like Gunner and Alix.

"Me neither," Travis replies.

And it hurts a little bit to hear it, even though I have no right to feel that way.

That night, we have a low-key evening. I make dinner, and then we settle in to watch a movie. My thoughts have been a jumble ever since we visited Alix and Gunner this afternoon. If Travis notices, he doesn't say anything. He's really good about letting me take things at my own pace, physically and otherwise.

The movie is some dumb action flick, and when it's over, I realize that pretty soon we'll be turning the lights out and going to bed. Suddenly, I know there's something I *have* to say to Travis, and the thought of going one more minute without doing it is absolutely unbearable.

"Travis," I choke out. "I need to tell you something."

He stops mid-rise from the couch and sits back down. "Okay. Shoot," he says, leaning back and crossing one ankle over his knee.

"No. I mean, I need to talk to you. About… everything."

One corner of his mouth lifts. "That's a hell of a lot of ground to cover. You might want to narrow it down a little."

But I can't bear to joke around about this. Not right now. I swallow the lump in my throat and look at him. Instantly, my eyes fill with tears. *Dammit, I don't want to cry when I do this. I have to pull it together.*

"Shit, is there something wrong?" he asks, alarmed. "You in pain? You need some Ibuprofen?"

"No, no," I say, shaking my head. "It's just…" I take a shuddering breath. "I need to explain why I left. I know I've already apologized. But I need you to know why I did what I did."

Travis's eyes cloud, but he nods once. "Okay."

"Please, just…" my voice sinks to a whisper. I clear my throat and try again. "Please just listen, and let me get through it. And try not to judge."

More than anything, I want the reassuring feel of Travis's touch right now. But I know I have to get through this whole thing first. And if he does touch me I'm sure I'll start bawling. So I scoot my body away from his about a foot, and turn toward him.

"You know I left on my eighteenth birthday," I begin, looking down at my hands. "And you know I stopped talking to you about a month before that." I gulp. "I know I never gave you an explanation, and I know you probably think I was mad at you. But I wasn't.

"You and I were getting… *closer*," I continue. "Closer to each other, and closer to… something I wanted and didn't want at the same time.

"I was afraid of sex. I think you probably knew that. But I wanted it, too." I pull my eyes up to his. "I wanted you, Travis. I did. My body wanted you. And I was getting closer to trusting you. And trusting that it would be all right when we had sex. That it wouldn't change anything — or at least that it wouldn't change anything for the worse.

"But what I didn't tell you was the reason I was afraid of sex." I break my gaze and look back down at my hands again. Even though I'm almost thirty years old, suddenly I feel like a child. "When I was a little girl, my stepdad would sometimes come into my room at night and touch me when he'd been drinking." Next to me, I hear Travis's sharp intake of breath. I force myself to rush on. "He never did anything more than just touch me, but it scared me. It made me scared to be alone with men. It made me feel like I couldn't trust *any* man to not be like that. Because I didn't know. He seemed like all the other dads and stepdads, on the surface. Most of the time, anyway.

"I never told my mom about it. I didn't know how. Eventually, she and my stepdad broke up, over something else. And then my mom died." I take in a deep breath, and let it out raggedly. *Here goes.* "And I got sent to foster care. And…"

My voice breaks. I've never told anyone this. I've never even said it out loud.

"And… I was afraid of Mr. Bonner. But at first I thought it was just me being paranoid. I thought it was just my imagination. But… then one night, when Mrs. Bonner was out… when I came home he jumped me, and… he raped me on the stairs."

"Jesus Christ, Brooke," Travis growls, but I shake my head furiously.

"No, no! Don't say anything! Otherwise I won't be able to get it out!" A sob cuts off my last word, and tears start streaming down my face. I fight to keep my voice, and keep going. "After that night, I was too afraid to face you again. I couldn't bear the fact that if I did, I'd have to tell you what had happened. And I knew I *would* have to, because I'd have to explain why I couldn't go any further. Why I couldn't let you touch me anymore. Because I couldn't stand it." I shake my head as the tears continue to come. "And I didn't want to ruin the only good thing that I had! And I didn't want you to think I was dirty, because if you did I would hate myself so much!"

I'm sobbing openly now, but I still have more to say. So I do, in ragged, wracking bursts. "I hated Mr. Bonner, for ruining us! And I hated myself, for being too afraid to trust you after that! I was afraid that if I let you go any farther, you'd do the… the same thing he had… I was afraid you'd rape me, too, and I knew it wasn't true, but I still couldn't get it out of my head!"

I bury my face in my hands and weep. Travis sits silently, thank God, and doesn't try to touch me. He lets me get it all out — all the pain I've been holding in for years. All the regret. All the remorse. He just sits there with me.

Finally, I manage to quiet my tears. I pull my hands from my face and force myself to look at him.

Travis's face is tortured. Pain, sorrow, and rage do battle in his features. But I know his anger isn't at me. It's at the past.

"I'm so sorry, Travis," I half-whisper. "I waited until my eighteenth birthday. Until it was legal for me to leave, and no one could stop me. And that's what I did." My eyes caress his face. "I didn't want to leave you," I moan. "But I had to. I loved you, Travis. I was so in love with you. I was just too afraid to be with you."

"Brooke," he rasps, his voice hoarse with emotion. "My God. I'm so, so fucking sorry."

"I wasted so much time…" I murmur. I squeeze my eyes shut against the pain of it all. "I know you were mad at me, Travis, and you had every right to be. I wish I'd been stronger. I wish I'd been strong enough to tell you."

"Brooke. Look at me," he says.

I open my eyes and tilt my tear-stained face toward his. He cups my chin in his hand. After so long without any physical contact, his touch makes me shiver.

"I was mad. Yes," he tells me. "Because I was fucking crazy about you. Losing you hurt like a bitch." He shakes his head and laughs softly. "Jesus, I'd never felt anything like it. I thought I'd never get over you. But the past is the past. And I'm not angry anymore." He gazes down at me. His blue eyes are soothing, like cool water. "But I'll tell you this. I'm not letting you go again. I'm not letting some piece of shit pervert waste one more second of our time."

Slowly, gently, his mouth comes down on mine. I answer his kiss eagerly, and like always, the intensity of it makes me dizzy. When he pulls away, I'm gasping. I reach up and hold onto his strong arms. They pull me toward him, enfolding me like a fortress.

"I love you, Travis," I whisper. "God, I've missed you."

"I love you, babe," he murmurs. "Now come on."

Then before I realize what's happening, I'm flying through the air. A second later, he's standing, and I'm in his arms.

"What are you doing?" I laugh, happiness flooding through me like a river.

"I'm takin' you to bed," he growls, heading for the bedroom. "We've got a lot of time to make up for, and I'm startin' right now."

That night, he takes me long and slow, even though I insist I'm mostly healed. But he's in control in the bedroom, just like always.

Afterward, I lie in his arms and listen to the night.

Wondering how, after all this time, I got so lucky.

I know from time to time, I'll look back and have to fight the sadness that comes with the knowledge that we spent so many years apart. But I also know Travis doesn't want me thinking like that. And in the end, maybe he's right. I'm with him now, and that's all that really matters. There was never anyone else for me, anyway.

And if I never let myself really get close to any other man, I think maybe it was because I was always supposed to be with Travis.

My Beast.

EPILOGUE
BEAST

Three months later

"I can't believe you're gonna make me live with a fuckin' guinea pig," I grumble.

"He'll grow on you," Brooke says cheerfully, handing me a box. "Now take this down to the truck, and I'll go get Walter."

I grab it from her, surprised at how heavy it is. You wouldn't think Brooke could lift it, from looking at her. But she's as tough as they come. It's one of the things I love best about her.

We've almost finished loading all the stuff from her place in Cleveland. We're driving back to Tanner Springs tonight, and officially moving into our new house. It's a rental, with the option to buy later. The place is in rough shape and needs a lot of work, but Brooke says she likes the idea of making it ours. And the landlord is more than willing to let us do the repairs. Free labor for him, after all.

When I get back upstairs from putting the last box in the truck, Brooke is just walking out of an apartment a few doors down, a medium-sized cage in her arms. She calls me over and introduces me to Lily, the little girl who took care of Walter the guinea pig for the past few months. Her mom, whose name is Gretchen, eyes me a little suspiciously, but tries not to look like she's checking me out. Lily openly stares at me, wide-eyed.

"You're like, a *giant*!" she breathes, and then snaps her mouth shut in alarm.

"Lily!" Gretchen hisses.

"It's okay," I chuckle. "That's one of the nicer things I've been called."

Brooke says her goodbyes, and promises to keep in touch. Downstairs, we load the guinea pig into the backseat of the truck and head out, leaving Cleveland in our rear view mirror. On the way out of the city, I glance over at Brooke. She's looking pensive, and a little sad.

"You gonna miss this place?" I ask.

"What? Oh, no. God, no," she laughs softly. "I was just thinking about Lily. How young she is, and how innocent still. I was just wondering if the other girls were like that. Before."

I don't need to ask who she means by the other girls. I know Brooke is still processing everything that happened with the trafficking ring. All of those girls are back with their families now. They're safe. But that can't erase what happened to them. Not completely. And I know that weighs on Brooke's mind.

"It could be, Brooke," I say gently. "But you had some bad shit that happened to you, too. It didn't destroy you, though. And it won't destroy those kids. They'll pull through, too."

"If they have people around them, to give them strength. And hope." Brooke looks over at me with her fuckin' gorgeous green eyes.

"You'll be doin' that soon, babe." I reach for her hand, and she slips it into mine. "You're gonna be raising generations of girls to be tough and strong and independent."

After Brooke resigned at the agency, she took a couple months to recover from her injuries and think about what she wanted to do next. I gave her time and space, and listened to her as she talked about wanting to help girls that might otherwise fall through the cracks. One day, I came home from the clubhouse and she was practically bouncing out of her skin with excitement. When I finally managed to calm her down, she told me she'd decided she wanted to open up a gym and fitness center for girls, specializing in martial arts and self-defense. With her FBI training, it was a perfect way to use those skills and teach girls empowerment and confidence in their physical abilities. She had this whole idea about opening a non-profit to offer scholarships to the ones who couldn't afford to be members. She wants it to be a place where any girl can go to feel safe, and strong, and wanted.

Ever since that day, she's been going full-speed ahead on getting this place up and running. The past couple weeks, she's been scouting out locations for rent that would be a good fit for what she had in mind. She's excited as hell, and I know she's gonna make this thing work.

I'm so fuckin' proud of her.

* * *

For someone who left Tanner Springs as soon as she was legally able, Brooke really takes to bein' back in town. Especially once we get Walter and the rest of her stuff moved in, it's almost like she never left. Of course, with the club women, she has a ready-made group of friends. She even starts going to Sydney's coffee shop a couple times a week, to hang out and work on her business plan.

As for me, I plan to make damn sure nothing ever makes her want to leave again.

And that included tracking down the last ugly remnant from her past.

I had Tweak trace the whereabouts of one Arlo Bonner for me. Turned out, Arlo and Renee Bonner moved out of Tanner Springs to a place a couple towns over, about five years after Brooke left. Mrs. Bonner passed away from lung cancer a couple years later, leaving Mr. Bonner a widower. The Bonners never had kids of their own, and Arlo was on disability and in poor health.

Brooke will never know what I did to Arlo Bonner. She doesn't need to know. The only important thing is, he's paid for what he did.

The law might never have caught him, but justice sure as fuck did.

* * *

I pull my bike into the garage after a long day at Twisted Pipes to hear music blaring at top decibel from inside the house. Opening the door, I see Brooke up on a ladder in the living room, painting the walls one of those weird muted blue-green colors that chicks always seem to have a precise name for. I go over to the stereo and turn down the volume, and she twists toward me in surprise.

"Oh! I didn't hear you come in!" she cries, setting her brush down on the top step of the ladder.

"You weren't gonna hear a damn thing, with the music so loud," I tease her. "Shit, I hope Walter likes Beyonce."

Brooke rolls her eyes. "That's not Beyonce. That's Alicia Keys."

I snort. "Whatever."

Back on the ground, Brooke comes up to me with a wide smile. "Do you like it?" she asks nodding toward the wall.

"It's good, babe. Whatever you want. Just don't make me put up with pink or some shit."

"So noted." Her mouth quirks up.

"You've got paint on your boob," I point out.

Brooke looks down at her black tank top. "Oh, you're right. Well, comes with the territory."

"You sure you didn't do that on purpose, to get me to look at your tits?"

She flashes me a saucy look. "Do I need paint to do that?"

"Hell no." I reach for the hem of her shirt.

"Excuse me, sir, what are you doing?" Brooke says in a coy voice.

"You're gonna get paint all over me," I complain, pulling the tank up and off her. "I have no choice."

Brooke pretends to protest, but she raises her arms up so the shirt comes off with no effort. Then she's standing there in front of me, naked to the waist and sexy as hell. My cock springs to attention.

"That's what I'm talkin' about," I growl. "Fuck, I'm starving for you, B. Have been all day."

"How can you be starving for me when it's only been about ten hours?" I pull her to me and she gasps as my mouth closes over one taut nipple. I don't bother to answer, because she should know by now. It's been this way ever since she stumbled back into my life. It'll always be this way. I can't get enough of her. It's like our bodies are making up for twelve years of lost time.

My tongue finds her pink bud, teasing it to hardness as she starts to moan. Her hands thread into my hair, gripping my scalp. "Oh, god, Travis," she whispers. "You're going to drive me crazy like that."

I know she's already wet for me. I know her body better than she does at this point. Sliding my hand under the fabric of her cut-off shorts, I find her slick folds with my fingers. She's soaked, just like I expected. My cock gets even harder. I was gonna take her upstairs to the bedroom, but I ain't got time for that. Instead, I reach up with my other hand and unbutton the shorts, yanking them and her panties off her in one motion. She's naked now, and ready for me.

Pulling her down on the carpet, I get my shirt off and flip her legs over my shoulders. Then, spreading her thighs wide, I move down between them and feast. Brooke's cries fill the house as I lick and suck. She's already swollen and needy, and

I'm in no mood to draw this out right now. I slide one finger inside her pussy, working her body and finding that spot inside her that drives her wild. Brooke tenses, her body ready to snap like a rubber band, and then explodes. Her orgasm rolls over her in waves as she bucks against my tongue. Jesus Christ, it's so fucking hot.

I pull her onto my cock as she's still coming, feeling the contractions of her pussy all around me. I pull out and then jackhammer into her, taking her hard like I know she loves. She calls my name, over and over, and I don't hold back. I shoot deep inside her, giving her everything I've got. God damn, it feels good to come inside her. I could do this every day for the rest of my life.

And I goddamn well intend to.

A few minutes later, we're lying back on the carpet, catching our breath. "That was quite a homecoming, Mister Carr," Brooke says, still breathing heavily.

"No shit. Like I said, I've been thinkin' about doin' that most of the day."

"I didn't manage to start anything for dinner," she tells me. "I wanted to get this room painted and I kind of lost track of the time."

"We'll order a pizza or something. You want to grab a shower with me first?"

"I'll shower later, after I'm done with this room. I should be able to get the rest painted in half an hour or so. Oh! By the way, I wanted to ask you about the third bedroom."

"Seriously?" I groan. "We're gonna talk about home decorating right now?"

"Come on, humor me," she laughs. "We still have to figure out what we're going to do with it. I've already decided I'm going to put a desk in the guest room, so that can be my office as well. But I don't know what to do with the other one. I don't do crafts, so that's out. And all your hobbies are too greasy to do inside."

I wait for a beat, considering.

"I got an idea," I murmur.

"Yeah?"

"You remember how I asked you if you'd ever thought about havin' kids?"

"M-hmm." She snuggles into my chest. "I said no. And if I remember correctly, so did you."

"Yeah. Well. It was true. I hadn't ever thought about it. *Then.*"

"And now?"

"Now, I think puttin' a baby inside you would be hot as hell." I put my hand on her flat stomach, lovin' how her body instantly responds to me.

"You do, do you?" she breathes. "You don't think when I'm a big pregnant lady you'll lose interest?"

The idea is so fuckin' ludicrous I burst into loud laughter. "B, you have got to be fuckin' kiddin' me. I've carried a torch for you for my entire adult life. You havin' my baby is just gonna make you sexier to me. Hell, bring on the wrinkles and gray hair." I lift my hand to her face and tilt her chin up so she's looking at me. "Every single thing that ever happens to your body from here on out is just gonna be a reminder to me of all the years that you've been mine. When we're eighty, seein' all those years on your face is just gonna make you more beautiful to me."

Brooke's eyes start to shine. She swallows and gives me a tremulous smile. "Why Travis Carr. Listen to you being all romantic."

"Damn straight," I growl. "Now about that baby. You in?"

She laughs, and a happy tear rolls down her cheek. "So, what you're saying is you want to make the third bedroom a nursery?"

"Well, yeah," I nod, shifting toward her. "But what I'm really sayin' is, if we're gonna have a baby, let's get to work."

I slip my hand back to her stomach, and then slide it further south. Brooke's breath catches in her throat when I find the spot I know she likes.

"You're insatiable, you know that?" she pants.

"With you, babe?" I growl as I move over her. "Always."

THE END

BOOKS BY DAPHNE LOVELING

Motorcycle Club Romance

Los Perdidos MC
Fugitives MC
Throttle: A Stepbrother Romance
Rush: A Stone Kings Motorcycle Club Romance
Crash: A Stone Kings Motorcycle Club Romance
Ride: A Stone Kings Motorcycle Club Romance
Stand: A Stone Kings Motorcycle Club Romance
STONE KINGS MOTORCYCLE CLUB: The Complete Collection

GHOST: Lords of Carnage MC
HAWK: Lords of Carnage MC
BRICK: Lords of Carnage MC
GUNNER: Lords of Carnage MC
THORN: Lords of Carnage MC

Sports Romance

Getting the Down
Snap Count
Zone Blitz

Paranormal Romance

Untamed Moon

Collections

Daphne's Delights: The Paranormal Collection
Daphne's Delights: The Billionaire Collection

ABOUT THE AUTHOR

Daphne Loveling is a small-town girl who moved to the big city as a young adult in search of adventure. She lives in the American Midwest with her fabulous husband and the two cats who own them.

Someday, she hopes to retire to a sandy beach and continue writing with sand between her toes.

Made in the USA
Middletown, DE
19 February 2019